HOIST THE FLAG

A TRIANGLES & TRIBULATIONS PREQUEL

Cover: Carol Marques
Logo/Group Header: Pretty In Ink Creations
Moral Support: Serenity Rayne, Sarah Klinger PA
Alphas: Sarah Klinger, Serenity Rayne, Chelsea Dawn
Sensitivity Reader: KC Bear
Editing/Formatting: Little Tailfeather Publishing

THANK YOU!

As an indie author, I appreciate your support more than you can imagine.

This has been my dream since I was a kid, and despite how it manifested, I'm so grateful to all of you for helping me make it happen.

I have a small request to make of you, dear reader.

If you find any kind of error—grammatical, developmental, typo, whatever—PLEASE DO NOT REPORT it to Amazon directly.

It hurts authors and their sales to do so—they pull our books until they deem it corrected—which kills our ability to work on new things or support ourselves.

Instead, please fill out this form: https://forms.gle/ASD1NTT6DJWfpLdq8

I will never be rude, angry, or anything but thankful if you come to me, I promise!

THANK YOU!

From the cockles of my black heart,

Cass

CONTENT WARNINGS

Content warnings are important and I don't ever want to harm a reader, so if you'd like more comprehensive warnings for any of my books visit: https://cassandrafeatherstone. com/series-by-cassandra-featherstone/

(This does get updated as I write, so it changes.)

This is a *paranormal whychoose romance with poly elements*. It is part of a larger universe that includes contemporary, but you do not have to read the other books to enjoy this one.

There are many situations included that are intended for mature audiences (18+).

In this book, there may be instances/references that could trigger some individuals such as: BDSM, past trauma, violence, booze, bullying, PTSD, body dysmorphia, bad language, impact play, body modifications, casual sex, mention of self-harm including suicide (not MCs), masturbation, voyeurism, objects used as toys, emotional abuse by family members and partners, and more.

Everything is <u>consensual</u>, except death.

Consent is ALWAYS sexy, and my MMCs will always seek it.

(Also, I don't kill animals. Fuck that.)

AUTHOR RAMBLINGS

This story came to me like many stories—while I was driving.

I left myself a note in my notes app so I could come back to once I finished one or any of my open series and didn't think about it again.

That is, until it came time to write a story for this Xmas anthology and I knew my original plan for a short story was no longer an option.

With much encouragement from a bunch of people, I pulled this idea out of the box, commissioned a cover, and write a blurb within a week. Carol really took my idea of Jack and ran with it, making a gorgeous rendition of our girl and an amazing theme for her series.

I sat down to write the tale from my blurb and disaster struck—as usual, my characters ran away with the plot and what followed is *so much more* than what I originally intended. A character who was meant to be temporary and a bit of a tongue-in-cheek nod at a well known story became a focal point. Relationships that weren't supposed to exist took root.

A path towards healing was found.

Now that I've finished the prequel, I'm more excited than ever to dive into the T&T world with Jack and her crew.

Her and Queenie's stories are so near and dear to me at this moment in life and they appeared at exactly the right time for me as an author and a person.

I hope you love them as much as I do.

Blood and guts,

Cass

NOTES FOR READERS

A few things you should know...

Given Jack's past and the world they live, there is foreign dialogue. I have made the *translations clickable end of chapter notes* to help.

This is multi-book series, so *everything will not be revealed in a prequel.* I promise it will all tie up with a HEA; don't worry!

There are some words that are slang, jargon, or foreign that may seem to be spelled wrong—*please use my form at the beginning of the book rather than report to Amazon* if you think something is wrong. It may not be and I want to make sure it doesn't get taken down so everyone can read!

Fictional people/organizations who are part of the *Legends of the Ouroboros* universe (but not this series) are mentioned. *If you haven't read their books, it won't keep you from enjoying this one.*

If you see this book *anywhere besides Amazon KU (in ebook format),* please reach out to me via social media. Pirating kills my ability to write full time and I am so grateful for your help.

A Note to My Loving Family Members and Friends...

Cassandra
FEATHERSTONE

<u>THANK YOU</u> FOR SUPPORTING ME BY BUYING MY WORK, BUT AS ALWAYS, I'M GOING TO SUGGEST YOU BOUNCE,

THIS IS SHORT INTRO TO THE FIRST BOOK IN A SERIES, BUT I DEFINITELY DO **NOT RECOMMEND** READING MY STORY. SOME OF THE OTHERS MIGHT BE OKAY, BUT MINE NEEDS COPIOUS CONTENT WARNINGS FOR THINGS YOU'VE NEVER HEARD OF.

RUN AWAY! I PROMISE YOU DON'T WANT TO GOOGLE SOME OF THE TERMS.

CAVEAT: IF YOU CHOOSE TO KEEP READING, KNOW THAT AT NO TIME WILL I EXPLAIN TERMS, POSITIONS, THEMES, TROPES, OR ANY OTHER PART OF THIS NOVEL AT FAMILY EVENTS, IN GROUP CHATS, OR ON SOCIAL MEDIA.

<u>DON'T ASK.</u>

HOIST THE FLAG PLAYLIST

CHAPTER TITLE SONGS

I make no apologies for how I chose to repair what you broke

— -MEREDITH GREY (*GREY'S ANATOMY*)

DEDICATION

To all the women who are
constantly looking at every
word, every sentence, and every
phrase with trepidation, hoping
they haven't chosen poorly...
May we live to see the day when our
tormentors get the justice they
so richly deserve.
Until then, you've got a friend
in me.

I

UNDER MY SKIN

JACK

OF ALL THE THINGS HUMANS INVENTED TO DESTROY one another—from torture implements to weapons of mass destruction—social media is by far the most insidious.

Sighing, I flick through my feeds on the bird app, then the influencer gram, and finally land on the clock app. I don't care if my volume is on high and the trending sounds echo throughout the room while I check up on my stats. A shudder runs through me when an icy tongue curls around my clit exactly how I like it. "Good girl, Queenie," I murmur distractedly when my body reacts to her efforts.

I know. Hashtag rude, right?

I shouldn't be so callous, but we both know the score here. My hand drops to her hair to pet the platinum strands gently and she damn near purrs. If only the royal court knew our secret, it'd be a scandal to end all scandals. Every muscle in my body clenches when she uses her magic to assist her fingers with filling me in every possible way. It's a ploy to get me to put down my

1

phone and pay attention to her as she services me. I can scent her desire from here, but she won't come until I permit it.

By the aroma in the room, she desperately wants to be given permission, and that's why I won't.

When I arrived in their kingdom centuries ago, her fresh faced sister had recently gotten coronated and her reign as Queen ended. While my girl swore this was entirely the best move for the kingdom, the wild magic she'd never been able to control rebelled. It didn't appreciate the demotion from Queen to keeper of the Enchanted Forest. The new queen and her consort were at their wits' end trying to figure out how they wanted to rule the kingdom, but since darling Queenie here kept making monsters accidentally, they couldn't get anything rolling.

I was tired of my latest gig—and to be honest, after that bitch Jill pushed me down a fucking mountain, I needed out of that toxic mess of a relationship—so I answered their ad on the supernatural slayer of LinkedIn. The royal couple advertised a position for a court advisor, but I soon found out they wanted a magical babysitter for their erstwhile relative. For decades, I struggled to clean up after her tantrums, listening to her sing that annoying ass song every time she fucked up, and then one day, it happened.

I yelled at her.

Not the brightest thing to do, I'll admit, but my career has been plagued by ill-advised actions that lead to nursery rhymes, songs, and now, TikTok videos of all my spectacularly poor decisions. I'm the most infamous Jack of all time and I hate it with the fire of the thousand suns that never shine in this arctic wonderland. Usually, my fuck-ups have to do with affairs of the heart, so despite what Queenie is currently working like a champ to do, I didn't get involved this time.

But I did figure out that putting the headstrong ex-ruler of the land into sub space—frequently—and fucking the shit out of her fixed the problem. Unusual problems often need out-of-the-box solutions, my friends. Since this one also meant I wouldn't have to go find outlets for my needs, I hopped on board—with stringent boundaries and rules. The last thing I needed was to turn the ex-Queen into a stage five clinger and get my ass shit canned when I broke her heart.

Part of my disastrous love life issues is my magnetic draw—the hint of succubi way back in my lineage is a gift that never stops giving.

"Jackieeeee," the icy queen whines with perfect timing. "I want to make you happy. Let me make you feel good without all of that silly work you're doing."

The clinger theory didn't work, by the way.

Sitting my phone aside, I peer down at her fondly. I care about her, even if I don't love her. Her supposedly 'kind, gentle' sister got a taste of power after her first year of ruling and now she's become a narcissistic monster that feeds on being cruel to others. Her princely consort is long gone and no one else will have her because the poison seeping from every word and deed is so toxic. Poor Queenie here spends most of her time avoiding the court because it makes her cry crystalline tears of sorrow when she talks about how it used to be before her sister went into full villain mode.

I'm her only ally and they pay me to be here—is there anything so sad?

"Queenie, I'm sorry I've been distant. I know you're worried about the party at the castle tonight. You're being such a good girl and I'm a bad Madame."

Her head lifts and her eyes widen with horror. "Merciful Odin, no! You are the one bright spot in the kingdom since she... burned down... my forest."

I forgot to mention that, right?

Earlier this year, my Queenie was at one of the bi-weekly 'attendance mandatory' parties her bratty sister throws for herself and she saw an old friend. Unfortunately, the *akhlut* wasn't attending the party as a guest; the Royal hunters tracked it down and captured it for the new queen's amusement. The poor creature was being forced to remain in its terrestrial form so it could hunt down enemies of the crown for sport.

To say she lost her shit would be an understatement.

It took weeks to thaw out the court, rebuild the castle to specifications, and confirm that the queen's 'pet' had escaped to the sea. While I was busy overseeing those efforts, Her Royal Bitchiness sent her army to burn down the Enchanted Forest and melt every single ice sculpture her sister made. It damn near destroyed my charge—I couldn't get her to do anything, even in subspace, except weep.

My punishment was also severe, but I wear the scars with pride. I refused to bind Queenie's magic, and I used connections all over the world to prevent her sister from getting another supernatural to do it. I even involved the Society, and they put her back in her place. After all, even the immortals of fairy tales and lore must bend to their will when they are unanimous.

That cost me, too, but I'm almost at the end of that sentence.

Four more weeks and I'm free to abandon my duties as keeper of this miserable prison of ice, snow, and cruelty. At the end of December, the agreed upon term expires and I'm taking off for sunny climes and complete retirement. No social media, no assholes teasing me about breaking my crown or being nimble and best of all, no more wielding frost magic for the nastiest royal narcissist I've ever encountered.

I haven't told Queenie that my time here is limited. The plan was to ease her into the idea of my absence while finding her a suitable Domme to meet her needs. I'd started looking for one via the *Obedience* app for supes, but after the forest fire... She's been far too fragile and I don't know how to broach it without an extinction level event.

It's not my job, really, but I've been here so long and she's come so far. I'm terrified her sister will hire a flunky with questionable morals to bind and imprison her when I go. The thought bothers the hell out of me on so many levels, but I can't put my finger on why. It has to be the top in me wanting to ensure my sub is safe and protected even when I'm no longer in charge of her.

Bollocks. Everything is a mess and it would be easier to find someone to take her beehive wearing ass out, so I'm certain Queenie is safe.

"Darling girl, why don't we curl up until it's time to get ready? I can feel your unease and I've not been doing a very good job of making sure you feel safe."

All traces of her magic leave my body, forcing a growl to escape my lips as the impending orgasm recedes.

Blast my soft heart. I gave myself blue ovaries—willingly.

"Really?"

I sigh again, flipping my head back on the pillows as I hold my arms out. No matter how fucking detached I try to be, I always do this shit. All my jobs end the same—a romantic disaster that could have been avoided if I hadn't let my pussy do the thinking. I'm hopeless... absolutely hopeless.

"Yes, love. Grab your Marshmallow and come here," I whisper.

"Can we call Trixie?"

My lips curve up and I give her a nod, watching as she puts her fingers to her lips and whistles. Within seconds, my thieving capuchin comes swinging into the room via the rope nets on the ceiling. Trixie drops onto the bed, dancing around for a moment before handing Queenie a pile of sparkling jewelry with a proud expression.

"Trix!" I admonish. I'm sure my monkey has pilfered her loot from many people around the summer castle and I'll be hearing about it from the guards any minute.

Queenie gasps when she opens up her hand, showing me the snowflake necklace. "My mother gave me this when they left for their trip. I... haven't had it in possession since long before your arrival."

Her whisper is full of awe and I narrow my eyes as I consider how carefully my girl spoke. "Why haven't you had a family heirloom that belongs to you for so long?"

"My sister confiscated it when we were little. She said she believed it was making my powers go crazy and had the guards lock it away."

Motherfucker. That bitch was always a sociopath; she scared everyone less because she wasn't freezing people to death by accident.

"Let me help you put it on." I take the fragile platinum chain and wrap it around her neck, settling the sparkling diamond and aquamarine encrusted charm between her breasts. "It looks lovely."

Queenie beams and snuggles into my side as she yawns. "Never more lovely than you."

Trixie chitters, giving me a reproachful look as I hold the now sleepy woman in my grasp. I roll my eyes back and stare up at the ceiling, wondering how I'm going to tell her I'm leaving without breaking her heart.

And maybe mine.

2

SWEET BUT PSYCHO
JACK

Looking around the obnoxiously over decorated hall, I sip my iceberg martini. You'd think the kingdom was flourishing and full of happy citizens if you saw a video of the affair on any of the supe social media, but that's not the case. I'm certain the new queen's social media attaché has posted a flagon of snippets to impress royals and plebs alike across the globe, but what they see online is definitely *not* the state of the people of the Ice Kingdom. It's heavily edited, perfectly lit freeze frame of how the upper echelon live crafted to portray Queenie's sister as a kind, supportive liege who loves her people.

Nothing could be further from the truth.

Anyone who spends time around her court of asskissers and hangers-on is well aware of how she actually feels about everyone —she spends hours gossiping and tearing apart those not in her inner circle. Whether the topic of the day is the peons below her or the royalty of other nations she's jealous of, my girl's sister is as venomous as a pit viper in private. However, at events in the public eye like this, the Queen dons her fakest smile and kindest demeanor in order to hide the darkness of her heart. I'm ashamed to say it took me longer than it should have to identify her two-faced behavior, but in my defense, they hoodwinked me into thinking I was a partner to the royal family. I provided balance that was much needed to help create a world where her people would thrive... or so she told me.

The minute I disagreed with her and the King-to-be, I became the enemy. I knew my charge wasn't being handled appropriately, and I refused to put her in the painful physical restraints they'd devised. It was unethical and cruel, but that didn't matter. Her Royal Bitchiness commanded it and if I didn't comply, they would have sent me packing before I even got the chance to try my own theories. I convinced them to give me leeway to experiment. Once I showed them I would obey, they left us alone in the summer palace.

I probably should have known then that the woman who seemed so concerned about 'helping' magic users like her sister learn to control themselves was only looking to protect her power.

Trumpets sound and I turn, watching the procession enter. They dressed Queenie in a ridiculously binding dress in ice blue and white. I pulled her platinum hair back in an intricate braid that falls over one shoulder. She's trembling under the layers of tulle, corset, and sparkling sequins—I can feel it. But the necklace Trixie found for her is still sitting over her heart, and I can only hope that it calms her enough to keep her power under wraps during this shitshow. I'm not allowed to accompany her in the slow walk to the thrones, though I'll be able to make my way over once the crowd has gone back to drinking and stuffing themselves full of the rich banquet.

The new Queen does not like competition for the affections of her cult.

That's why my girl is tied up in knots and fluffy body obscuring skirts; she's soft and curvaceous, with an ample bosom and round ass. She looks like Bettie Page but softer and blonder. In contrast, her sister is thin, with curly red hair often styled in a large beehive. Her sharp features are always watching and she frequently outfits herself in designs like she's wearing this evening: a long, svelte purple dress with a high collar at the neck and no back to speak of. I've seen pictures of them both as children, and while Queenie looks exactly like the girl who locked herself away, her sister has morphed into a harder version of herself since the coronation.

They're both beautiful women—I'd never body shame another woman to make myself feel better, especially in public. I can't say the current Queen would be as respectful, despite her many social media posts claiming the opposite. But despite all the vitriol and punishment her sister doles out, Queenie loves her sister dearly and would be disappointed in me if I pointed out the hypocrisy practically oozing from the pores of our ruler. It frustrates the living fuck out of me because one of my grand plans for leaving was to use the dirt I've gathered on the phony Queen of the Ice Kingdom to knock her out for good.

Okay, that plan was in direct opposition with my plan to keep my girl safe, but truthfully, I can't stand liars and fakes.

Speaking of the two-faced snot, she's finally alighted from the dais and is now standing in front of the crowd. As usual, they filled the room with sycophants and toadies who will hang on her every word as if it came from the lips of the gods themselves. They all directly benefit from her favor—for now—so they're eager to cheer and clap, even when the words coming out of their liege's mouth are dripping with hatred and anger.

"My devoted followers," she says as she looks directly into the camera in front of her. Her perfectly coiffed assistant flutters around the dais, adjusting lights and watching her with adoring, brainwashed eyes. I'm ready to barf when she continues. "Thank you all for coming to celebrate my dear friend Bianca's ascension to Ladyship. I couldn't be more pleased to grace all of you with my presence on this momentous occasion."

Yikes. The ego on this woman is out of control.

The diminutive Bianca alights the steps and kneels in front of the queen like a feudal serf. I can tell by the look on my Queenie's face that she's dismayed, but I don't know why. It's time to move. If her upset is too overwhelming, we're going to have an incident live streamed to every supe community around the world. I won't be able to protect her from the things her sister wants to do if she's caught on camera losing her shit.

Of course, that's probably that petty bitch's plan—to show the entire world she's the victim rather than the other way around.

You'd hope people who develop their own powers as children or teens would understand, but over the millennia, I've learned that both humans and supes only see what they want to see. If admitting the truth doesn't directly benefit them, they're happy to allow tyrants to flourish in their midst. It's even harder to move their opinions if they are being spoon-fed sob stories in the background, so I assume the Queen's 'flying monkeys' have been working in the shadows to make this set-up palatable.

Trixie appears out of nowhere, chittering her outrage as she absorbs some of the anger flowing through me from our companion bond. Like most of her kind, she's quite empathetic with me and we're able to communicate handily in that manner. I turn my head briefly, nodding at her, and she scampers off quickly. I sent her in search of a distraction if need be, but while she's doing so, I'm quietly making my way to my girl.

"Arise, Lady Bianca of the Ice Kingdom. The fealty you and your family have shown since the start of my reign will now be rewarded. Your farms will become part of the royal proffer and all the realm will know we support your goods. May all of my kingdom enrich your coffers and make your name legend within the bounds of our borders."

Queenie's eyes widen again, and I can tell she's struggling. The stamp of royal approval will encourage the courtiers and the wealthy to shift their purchases to garner the queen's favor. It will leave farmers across the kingdom with rotting fields and unpaid taxes—a dangerous combination for a citizenry that is barely scraping by while the idiots attending this party are living high on hog. Sadness is coming off of my charge in waves; she didn't give up her crown for her sister to turn their rule into a dictatorship.

Bianca does as she's bidden, turning to smirk at the cameras. Her family was financially sound and their businesses were already flourishing. There was no need to do this, but the new queen did it simply to make my girl upset while the video rolls. Everyone knows the monstrous Business Guild is filled with the Queen's pets, so their decision to publicize a formal ceremony that has already happened was strategic. Nothing about the ceremony today is real—it's all a giant PR move and an attempt to provoke Queenie into signing her own death warrant.

By the time I make it backstage, the queen is droning on about her various causes—none of which she gives an actual damn about—and patting herself on the back for being a 'philanthropist'. She's not fooling anyone; the artists and merchants she's withdrawn her support from if they eclipsed her influence have damn near had to go into Witness Protection. A few of her former assistants have literally disappeared off the face of the earth rather than face the ire of the Ice Queen.

Luckily for me, her vanity knows no bounds. I'm neither thin nor curvy and because of the uniqueness of my features, they have relegated me to wearing a courtier get up that matches my charge's clothes. The breeches and corset are in complementary blues and my shirt is white as snow. It washes out my pale complexion, but I don't care. Because they did not force me into some loathsome gown, I'm able to slip through the curtains stealthily and place myself behind Queenie with ease.

I place a hand on her shoulder and I can feel the temperature in the room rise slowly as her breaths even out. She's counting them, probably even naming how many things she can touch, taste, smell, see, and hear in an effort to calm her frayed nerves. *This* is the woman I came to know after I found the solution to her magic fueled tantrums all those years ago.

The ex-queen cares deeply about her people and this stunt has her heart flossing with worry.

Watching the cameras move for a moment, I plot their paths so I know when I can lean down to whisper in her ear without being seen on the stream. When they pass, I murmur low against the shell of her ear, "You're doing wonderfully, darling. Keep breathing and know that if this gets further out of hand, I poised Trixie to cause a commotion that will allow for your exit."

My simple reassurance pulls the rest of the tension out of her frame and I watch as the charm on her chest glows for a second, then dims.

Narrowing my eyes, I make a note to examine it more closely when we are back at the summer castle. Magical items are both a blessing and a curse—while I don't believe the psycho was right to relieve my girl of her heirloom, I also don't want anything amping Queenie up.

I've long believed that my icy lover may be the product of something other than the happy marriage all the stories speak of. Her sister was fully human until she became a fairy tale creature and neither of their parents had been documented as having magic. If they had, my girl would have had *some* training prior to their deaths. Instead, she was left to founder on her own with no discernible support system to help her learn control. Her shame and fear were multiplied when she grew older and could not hide her gifts.

No supernatural parent would allow their child to become a danger to their own kingdom.

My dealings with the local Council and the Society only increased my doubts about her heritage. They were far too willing to bargain with me for her freedom and their price for helping was extremely low. The leaders of *my* kind definitely know something they are not willing to share about the daughters of this kingdom.

If my suspicions are accurate, Queenie may be a lost one and that means finding out her true parentage is the only way to truly harness her powers.

The question remains... Does her sister know? If so, was turning my girl into a monster her plan all along?

The speech ends and the applause begins, filling the room with shouts and cheers as the redhead pretends to be humble and embarrassed by the praise. It's hard to see unless you are as close as I am now, but the glint in her eye is telling.

She never intended to be anything but the center of attention and Queenie was in her way.

I can't leave her here without protection or she'll be dead within a week.

3
ESCAPE
JACK

AFTER THE DEBACLE AT THE PARTY, I SPENT MOST OF the night keeping a *very* close watch on Queenie. She mingled as required, danced with a few clods who were brave enough to approach her, and kept a healthy distance from her sister. I asked her to make certain she was far enough away to keep the petty despot's gaze off of her in hopes there wouldn't be consequences for how lovely my girl looks despite the obvious effort to make her self-conscious. Even with the constraints of her bulky gown and tightly cinched corset, Q floats across the floor with royal bearing—something her sister has never achieved. It's not something you can teach, regardless of the many human movies eschewing the notion.

Carrying yourself with the confidence and grace of a truly powerful woman is something genuine leaders are born with—no amount of personal success or financial gain can trump natural gifts.

That's another reason I'm stuck on my theory about Queenie's origins. She doesn't move or think like a human, even though she's been surrounded by them for the entirety of her life. Every-thing she does screams 'square peg in a round hole' and I believe that's why I was able to identify a solution for her uncontrollable magic so quickly. Whatever supes she's descended from abso-lutely feed off of emotions or sex or energy. The options are wide open after that because I'm uncertain if she may have more abili-ties. She's never explored simply because she doesn't *know they exist.*

When one of the ass-kissing court members delivered the message that we could leave the ball, I scrambled to find my charge. She was laughing softly as she spoke with someone on the waitstaff, waving her hands as she gestured around her. Trixie was perched on the table nearby, keeping a watchful eye on Queenie, just in case. As I approached, the capuchin chit-tered happily and my girl turned to give me a bright smile. Leave it to the former queen to be chatting up the servants rather than listen to some wealthy fuckwit in her sister's echo chamber drone on about how well the kingdom is doing now. It hurts her to hear given that we pass the villages where the common citi-zens live on the way to the summer palace and they are *not* doing well.

We can't do a damned thing about it, though. Her Royal Bitchi-ness would happily destroy Queenie's reputation in the kingdom and across the globe if we spoke out about her abusive behavior. I've spun the situation in every permutation, trying to figure out how to leak the truth in a way that won't get my girl imprisoned in some dank dungeon and my ass tried for treason. The knowledge that her sister has spies everywhere and has been playing the victim far longer than anyone could imagine limits our ability to share the authentic version of events.

Fear is her weapon despite the image she's built in public of the delightful, kind woman who cares about all of her realm.

"Your sister behaved this evening," I murmur to Queenie as the carriage continues towards our home.

Her smile is full of sadness as she turns away from the window to glance at me. "Her announcement will destroy all the other farmers. They cannot sell their goods and fall behind on their taxes. We both know what she does to those who don't pay their tribute to her."

I do, and it's why I plan every single moment of events we attend in her presence.

"The scars on my back say I do, darling. Any dissension in her ranks, whether willful or unintentional, will be punished swiftly and cruelly." I pause, choosing my words carefully. "Yet you struggle to hear that she's not the sister you recall from your youth or from before the coronation."

"I..." Queenie lifts her hands to her face and draws a shuddering breath. "I feel as though my issues are to blame for the changes in her. Dealing with me and my messes made her hard because she had to worry whether she might have to do something terrible to stop me."

I snort, shaking my head slowly. "Fuck that, Q. Plenty of human families raise magic users without forcing them to isolate, stealing their kingdom, and threatening to imprison them with magical restraints. Since Trixie found that necklace, I'm questioning the memories you have of your childhood with her. Maybe you've idealized them to cope with the trauma."

"Idealized?" Her brow furrows, and she closes her eyes, growing still. I almost ask what she's doing, but then she finally whispers,

19

"The day she took the necklace, I borrowed one of her dolls so I could have a tea party with mine. When she came to retrieve her doll, she was very upset. She took the necklace, saying if I took something of hers, she should be able to take something of mine. I lost control and then she told our guards that they should lock it away because it caused my magic to misbehave."

Of fucking course she did, the bratty little snotsucker.

"Queenie, your sister took the one thing your parents gave you before they disappeared because you borrowed a toy. She made *sure* no one would ever give it back to you by lying about what caused your powers to flare. The Queen of the Ice Kingdom is a sociopath, and she *enjoys* making you and everyone else suffer."

Tears fill her eyes and she looks out the window for a moment before replying, "I've tried not to see it. All I have left is my sister and when I got control of my magic briefly and ruled the kingdom, we felt so close. It was what I'd always longed for. After I gave up the throne, it was hard to admit it was all for show. She'd shown me everything she needed to in order to get what she wanted from me. Once she had it, she morphed into a person I'd pretended didn't exist."

I've never heard her be quite this honest about her sister and their past, but I think the appearance of this mystery necklace has something to do with it.

The Ice Kingdom doesn't have magic users outside of my girl, but I'm wondering if maybe the so-called advisors and the current queen consulted one. It wouldn't be hard to find a witch, mage, or hell, even a djinn for hire on the supe side of LinkedIn or Fiverr. Many magic users are traveling Swiss Army knives and sell their services to the highest bidder regardless of the request. Once Queenie emerged from her room and took her place as the ruler of the kingdom, they may have realized she would never allow the iron-fisted tyranny they have in place now.

"Is it possible you can see more clearly since Trixie gave you the necklace from your parents?" I ask. I know my girl isn't very familiar with the outside world and definitely doesn't know about the variety of supes and beings beyond the walls of her kingdom, but if I can trigger a memory about when she received it or something that was said, I might puzzle out if it really is a part of this.

"You know... things seem sharper. Like when you put on glasses and your eyes work better—or so I'm told."

"That makes perfect sense, darling." I tug her into my side, mulling over her metaphor as the scenery flies by. "I wonder if that has something to do with your memories and your perception of the queen being less... forgiving."

The look on her face is one of pure horror, and it hurts my heart when the shock fades into pain. "You think she would do that?"

Hell yes, I do. That woman has probably been scheming from the second your parents went missing.

But I can't say it that way because Queenie looks like she's going to crumple as it is. If I'm going to propose she comes with me when I leave, I need her to be strong and determined, not struggling through the stages of grief as she admits who her sister really is. "I don't know, pet, but I think it's likely the necklace is tied to your wonky powers. Everything else is mere speculation."

"What can we do? I have it back for now, but if our suspicion is true, she'll try something else," she whispers as she wipes the tears. "I'll have to spend the entirety of my life locked in that castle, so I don't give her anything to use against me."

I'll be damned; she figured it out on her own.

I give her a small smile and hold my fingers to my lips before I speak. "We can talk when we're at home. I'm able to check for unwanted guests in our room—I don't trust that spies aren't everywhere."

Queenie scoots closer and presses against my side. As I stroke her hair, I close my eyes and laugh internally. That I was going to find someone to care for her and go on my merry way was ridiculous. My previous cock-ups always centered on getting involved with someone and it going spectacularly wrong. I'm incapable of maintaining the emotional distance I lecture myself about internally and pretending otherwise was folly.

This woman is yours now, Jack, and whether or not you planned for it, you're going to have a stowaway on your journey.

"Is it clear?"

I point the magic compass at the last section of the room, waiting to see if it lights up. I inherited this damn thing from a saucy pirate I had an affair with during a vacation in the 1700s, and it's usually pretty accurate. My collection of magical curiosities is vast—I always take a souvenir of my failures as a reminder of what not to do the next time. It's never actually *helped* until now, but I'll be damned if I'm not patting myself on the back.

Story and fairytale immortals are an interesting breed. We keep the powers we had originally and gain whatever mythos the humans tack on as our story grows. Some of my former incarnations were human, and some have been magical, so I have a myriad of abilities. I couldn't manipulate ice or snow until I came here to take up the mantle of Jack Frost.

That my name is Jacqueline has been inconsequential over the years. I'm stuck with Jack no matter what I do.

"Jackie?"

She's the only person in history I've ever allowed to call me that, and it's only when she's worried. "It seems so, love. I've got Trix out scanning the castle books and crannies with my amulet. I want to know if there are rogue spells lurking about anywhere else as well."

"We can talk in here, though?" Her brow creases with worry and I nod. "The idea of Chelle actively trying to hurt me since we were kids is... really hard."

I tug her into my arms, tucking her head beneath my chin. Queenie is tall, but I'm half Fae, half giantess, so I'm still taller. "I know. I don't talk about the past often, but there have been people who damaged me in that way. Jill, Galen, Natalia... all of them almost destroyed me at different points in my life. They weren't my sister, of course, but I loved them with all of my heart and they turned out to be unworthy of that. Chelle is one of the most insidious liars I've encountered in a while; it's not surprising she could fool you for so long. She used your soft heart and giving nature to her advantage."

A sob shivers through my girl and I realize she's at the beginning of an arduous journey through grief.

Right now, she'll be in denial—the death of the person she believed her sister and best friend to be is hard to accept. It will be a constant source of self-doubt and recrimination in her heart and mind until something concrete makes it undeniable. Then she'll be angry as the fire of her betrayal rages through her and once she calms, she'll try to make a deal with the universe if she can have her back. After that will come depression and finally acceptance. I'll need to be her support system as she runs the gamut of emotion and since I never had one when I went through it, I will make sure she never ends up in the clutches of that spiteful woman again.

"She doesn't care about m-me. All she wanted was someone to scapegoat and beat up on until she could steal what was rightfully mine. And she doesn't give a single fuck about our kingdom—only the power and wealth that comes with it."

Truer words. Everything the current queen does serves her enormous and undeserved ego.

"Yes, but once we escape, everyone will see her for the fraud she is." Q lifts her head and looks at me in confusion. "She's a one-trick pony without your magic, my love. Chelle isn't like you—she's not gifted or special—when you aren't here to support her with your magic, she'll have to use money and fear to force people to pay attention to her. She doesn't have friends; she only has acolytes and enemies."

After she hiccups and wipes her nose, she shrugs and mumbles, "You mean she won't be able to blame the bad things on me and people will see her for who she really is?"

I tap her nose, smiling fondly. "Exactly. Without you to take her fury out on, she'll attack the minions surrounding her instead of hiding her true face. Then she'll lose what power she has and the masses won't be able to deny how truly despotic she is. She might even melt down in public and destroy her fake image all on her own."

I want to be there to see it, but protecting my girl's mental health and freedom is more important.

"How do we break free? She has spies everywhere; we can't trust anyone to listen or help us."

Queenie isn't wrong—the queen holds onto her power by swindling everyone in her circle by love bombing them. It's not a superpower, but it's a really goddamn effective one. People will always look for what benefits them the most and her narrative has only spread since she took the crown.

"I don't know yet, my love. I need to spin the board around for a bit until I can see the right moves. Each step must be carefully weighed and considered before we take it."

"When do you think we'll leave? Where will we go? I've never been farther than the neighboring kingdoms and they aren't likely to cross my sister."

Shit. Now it's time to have a tough conversation and in her current state, it's going to be harder than it would have been before.

"I have something to tell you."

Here goes nothing...

4

SANCTUARY

QUEENIE

THE LOOK ON JACKIE'S FACE WORRIED ME AND ONCE she started divulging the events of her past, I knew why she grew so serious. She's *much* older than I am and the breadth of her experience dwarfs my knowledge of the world. Even before our tale became the stuff of legends, my fairytale creature status made aging infinitely slower than other beings. We exist in partial stasis for much of our lives, allowing our tales to gain notoriety over many generations. Her existence in multiple rhymes, tales, and cultures means she's lived many centuries longer and survived more than I ever realized.

This is the first time she's opened up about all of her past posts and it's quite daunting.

"When you were Nimble, your companion was a vampire named Galen and his twin, Trace. He blamed you for his arson habit and then they cheated on you with a leprechaun and a pixie?"

Her lips curls up in disgust. "Yes. I almost ended up in a supe mental hospital afterward."

"And before that, you were with a gorgon named Natalia who got you both cursed with eating disorders because she insulted a demigod?"

Jackie sits up, holding her arms out. "You see what now? That's normal for someone with giant's blood. I'm curvy, thick, muscled, and over two hundred pounds. After Nat's bullshit, our curse was to become the opposite of our natural selves. She gained a hundred fifty pounds, and I dropped to a little over a hundred. She couldn't stop eating and I couldn't stop dieting. That motherfucker she pissed off had a sick sense of humor."

I blink. I can't imagine what Jackie looked like so thin and frail. She's perfect exactly how she is—no matter what insensitive remarks my sister has made in public over the years. Her frame is solid and comforting when I need it, but soft and warm as well. At that weight, she'd be a skeleton. "It's hard to picture. You must have been miserable."

"I was. Nat and I weren't very good for each other anyway, but I hadn't realized it yet. The curse simply amplified our differences. She did nothing but hide and bemoan her fate, but she wouldn't seek the asshat out and apologize. The only way I became exempt was when I finally left her."

"The other mess—the one not long before you came here—was Jill?"

She swallows hard and nods. "Jill was the most painful. It's why I showed up here, determined to allow no one into my heart again."

I will not like this; I can feel it.

"Jill..." My love gathers her knees to her chest, hugging them as if she needs to protect herself before she continues. "I've dated many species and genders over the years. Jill was the first human. Her mother was a vengeance demon and her father was human. When her mother killed her father for gambling away their family fortune, Jill was only ten."

"That's very sad, but I don't understand why that matters," I say softly. "My parents died when I was... oh."

Jackie nods and gives me a sad smile. "None of that was kept from her and her mother took her along on her 'business' as a child. She spent her entire life seeing the worst in every person she encountered—both as targets and clients."

I place my hand on her knee. My strong, capable defender is trembling like a leaf in the breeze. Whatever she did to help herself get through this pain did not heal entirely. The fear is radiating from her in waves that are spiking against my magic. Even her tone of voice is less confident.

"Growing up with a parent who has a severe mental disorder is very difficult and warps the child's love map. Or... that's what the therapist told me when I took the job of being her guardian. Her mother made me visit Jill's doctors before I accepted the job to ensure I had a realistic expectation of how difficult my position as guardian would be." A single tear runs down her cheek and she swipes at it. "I didn't believe a human could be capable of being so dangerous to someone with my magic and experience. That was my first mistake."

"What happened, Jackie?"

"The manipulation her doctors warned me about was as powerful as any magic. She spent the first few months working her way into my heart and mind by putting on the perfect mask.

We even started a wildly popular YouTube show together called *Jack & Jill* that made us internet famous." Her head drops to her knees and a muffled sob echoes in the room. "Once she had me hooked, that's when she turned the screws. Her shower of love, affection, and support were all a ploy to find my weak spots. I shared all my past pain, my insecurities, and my dreams with her. And then she used them to break me down, little by little, until I was a shadow of myself. "

My eyes fill with ice and the temperature of the room drops by twenty degrees as anger courses through me. I can't allow Jackie to stop to comfort me, though, so I touch the necklace with my free hand, hoping she's right about its power to soothe my magic. "Tell me the rest, love."

"Once I was under her thumb, I wasn't her friend or confidant or lover anymore. She molded me into her plaything—a vessel for either making her feel good about herself or a victim of her fury whenever anything in the world made her angry. If someone criticized her or her mother behaved like the sociopath she was, I endured her pain—emotionally at first, but as time went on, physically, too." Jackie looks up for a moment with red eyes, biting her lip as she waits for it to dawn on me.

The scars.

My rage propels me off the bed, and swirls of ice and wind fill the room. When my feet lift off the ground, I know my eyes have gone wintery white, and it covered my hair in snowflakes. The Queen of Ice and Snow in her full glory is not something many people have witnessed, but the power is flowing over my skin like an old friend. When I finally speak, my voice is a loud, booming demand. *"Where is she? I will wrap her in ice until each of her limbs falls off and her organs turn to popsicles. No one is permitted to harm what belongs to the Snow Queen!"*

"Holy shit, Q," she whispers in awe. "You... I've never seen your magic like this. You're floating and I'm pretty sure you might be freezing the entire castle."

"Jackie! Tell. Me. Where. She. Is." I can't seem to curb the magic emanating from my pores, nor can I focus on anything but destroying the woman who hurt my love so deeply.

"I don't know, Queenie. I have to tell you the rest of my story for you to understand. But you gotta calm down, or this is going to draw attention we don't want."

I suck in a breath and close my eyes, picturing my magic coming back to me instead of pushing out into the world. It's the technique Jackie taught me and it usually works with the small bursts, but I don't know if it's going to with this amount of power.

Her voice is soft as she continues. "Everyone knew we were a pair, and we were quite the social media darlings. Jill was very careful to keep her mask on in public—so she looked like the most amazing partner I could have when everyone was paying attention. All her cruelty was behind closed doors, even the nasty scars on my backs from her favorite knives. Her mother turned her into a psychopath and I should have asked more questions in the beginning about why her previous partners were no longer around."

A bolt of ice shoots from my fingers at that statement and I watch as it shatters the mirror above our dresser. *How dare that woman convince Jack she was at fault for not realizing she'd committed to a sadist?* Another deep breath allows me to curl my fists to prevent my magic from lashing out again, and I nod for her to go on.

"By the time it got that bad, I couldn't figure out why no one could see all of her subtle and not-so-subtle abuse. I tried to find help, but no one wanted to see the famous Jill from the *Jack & Jill* show as anything but the quirky, funny persona she'd built. I ended up so depressed that I thought my only way out was to cut all ties. I went to her mother and requested to be let out of my contract—I even offered to buy it out. She refused. Having me around meant she didn't have to deal with the monster she created, and she said I would have to stay until the contract ended in two years."

Jackie's face darkens, and the room goes silent. "So I had to wait to escape my abuser. It was both a blessing and a curse that Jill's mother informed her of my request. Her outrage at my attempt to save myself caused her to lose control of the carefully maintained facade, even in public. It started small—vague insults that only I would understand—but by the end, she graduated to more hurtful things, like fat shaming, accusing me of using her, and insulting my abilities. It was like the public 'good Jill' and the private 'evil Jill' melded into a bitter shell of the woman I thought I knew."

Five things I can see, four things I can touch, three things I can smell, two things I can hear, one thing I can taste... blood from biting my tongue.

"It got worse and worse. No one called her out on it and I knew if I said anything, she'd twist it and make me the villain. I stayed quiet and took the blows so I could finish the deal and move on without her destroying my reputation anymore than she already had. That is... until the implosion." Jackie sighs and runs her hair through her silvery strands, the weight of what's coming making her look utterly defeated.

"The implosion?" I ask carefully. My feet haven't touched the ground yet, but I've been controlling my magic better than ever before, so I don't ruin our chances of getting away. It's hard, but I'm managing—for now.

"We hadn't started filming season two because of all the problems. I was a mess of anxiety and depression, so I couldn't bring myself to even try to work on it, but we had to keep up appearances for the fans, so the advertising continued. One night, we were at a media event for the show and a reporter approached us with questions that suggested my popularity with the fans was increasing. He didn't say Jill was *less* popular—everyone knew she had her own little armada of 'Jillies'—but he *said* the polling showed I was gaining my own fan base."

Considering the way my sister behaves when our people talk to me instead of worshiping her, I know what's coming and why Jackie knew about her before I did.

"She had a total meltdown in front of the entire party and they kicked out us. The next day, the footage was everywhere, and everyone saw the person I saw in private on every platform imaginable. Advertisers and fans abandoned her like moldy bread. I knew the show was dead, and I hoped she'd talk her mother into kicking me to the curb. When she asked me to meet her in her room, I thought she was going to fire me, but that's not what happened."

My hand shoots back to the snowflake necklace, praying to Freya that it works because I know this is the worst part.

"I found her on the balcony, waiting for me with a smile that reminded me of the old Jill. The discussion of the future of the show was fairly normal until I made the mistake of mentioning how thoroughly the media had covered her tantrum. She did not

CASSANDRA FEATHERSTONE

like the notion that it couldn't be saved. That's when she grabbed me and threw us both off the balcony."

I can't help but gasp, and a flurry of snowflakes fills the room. "She did *what*?"

"We were pretty high in the fortress, so the ground came flying at us fast. I did everything I could to cushion the fall, but…" My love turns away, looking at the shattered mirror. "I survived and Jill didn't. Her human body was too fragile and mine was damaged, but not destroyed. When I got out of the hospital, my things were boxed and shipped to my brother's house and the media had received the note she emailed before I got to her room. She accused me of everything she'd done to me and hinted she feared for her life. One final manipulation almost landed me in jail, but luckily, there was no proof of which one of us was lying. I ran as far as I could, covered myself in tattoos to remind me of why I shouldn't ever get involved with a client, and waited until it all blew over to look for jobs again."

My poor, scarred Jackie. No wonder she acted like she did until now—she's terrified to allow herself to care for anyone.

She turns to face me, and all the rage dissipates from my body. My feet land on the ground and the ice disappears as I watch the tears roll down her cheeks. Her pain is so palpable that I can feel it vibrating in the air like a force unto itself. It's obvious she blames herself for all of it and has never healed the trauma that crazy bitch caused.

That stops now.

"You were going to finish your job here and leave me, weren't you?" I ask as the reason for her deeply personal confession comes to me.

"Yes."

I walk over and wrap my arms around her, burying my face in her neck. "Now we're going to escape this frozen hellhole together."

Even if I have to kill my sister to accomplish it.

5

WHO ARE YOU?

JACK

I DIDN'T EXPECT QUEENIE TO TAKE MY ADMISSION AS well as she did, but I also didn't plan for a blizzard inside our bedroom. Once she calmed down and I could get my shit together, we started plotting. By the time we fell asleep, I felt like we were truly working as a team for the first time.

That was a week ago and in the interim, the preparation for the Yule celebration began. Though the Ice Kingdom is perennially covered in sparkling holiday snow and ice, the royal family makes an enormous show of decking the halls. My girl is a big part of that effort because of her magic, so she's been creating sculptures and icicle garlands day and night. Her sister has guards accompany us to each location, watching from the shadows as Q does her thing.

At first, I thought we'd been discovered, but the lack of punishment dispelled that notion. When a couple of children tried to approach us in the village, the escorts shooed them before they could get within fifty yards of us. I realized Chelle is terrified we will speak to the people of the realm—something I've never seen happen before. It made me wonder why it changed and what she's hiding.

I told Queenie that I needed to do recon on my own. If there's trouble in the villages, it might give us an escape route. Anything that might distract the current queen or derail her holiday celebration is fair game when it comes to getting the two of us very far away from the Ice Kingdom.

In order to find out what's happening, Trixie and I are sneaking out of the underground tunnels below the castle. The capuchin is riding on my shoulder, keeping quiet as I use the same compass I did in our room. Its needle spins as I slog through the muck, eyes darting at every noise. I don't believe the queen assigned guards to watch these tunnels, but I have no idea how deep her paranoia runs.

Of course, that paranoia is less chuckle-worthy now that Queenie and I are planning our subterfuge.

"Wah wah wah!" The rumble call Trixie makes gives me immediate pause. Capuchins make it when something they hear is dangerous or scary, including my little friend. Just because I didn't hear what she did doesn't mean it's not there.

Moving slowly so I don't step on any debris or slosh a puddle, I sink into the shadows of an archway and listen. After a few moments, the sound of heavy boots echoes off the stone and laughter resonates around me. Plastering myself against the wall, I peek out to see who is stomping around the secret tunnels of our castle.

"Aye, Jorge, we plundered a bountiful feast, mate!"

"For the love of Poseidon's salty ballsack, *please* leave the pirate slang for the ports. We get enough of it when the crew's about."

38

Who the fuck are those guys and what are they doing in our home?

"I will when you promise to embrace our latest venture. I'm trying to get you in the spirit of the yo-ho-holidays, mate."

"How can I do that when you *insist* on calling me by the wrong name?"

"Don't be cranky, Jorgie. I only do it to get your scales ruffled, so after we distribute this loot to the people of the village, you'll be inclined to put *me* in your mouth rather than your tail."

That makes my brows raise and I scoot closer to the light, hoping to make out these two thieves without getting caught. They sound cute and I've always been a fan of bad boys. The playful one reminds of someone I knew a long time ago—the pirate I got the compass from. He was human when we dated, so it's not likely to be him, but I've often missed his whimsy.

A brief scuffling sound is followed by a groan. I ease into the light, squinting for a moment until I can make out the pair pressed against the tunnel wall. The one I assume is Jorgie has black and green spiky hair, tattoos on his face and neck, and a lip ring made of shiny obsidian. He's holding a burly redhead against the wall while he strokes his... tentacles?

This kind of shit only happens to me, I fucking swear.

Queenie would quite like having two shifter hotties join us, I think. She doesn't have any experience with anyone but me, but her adventurous streak has led us to watch people in the past. We enjoy a bit of voyeurism and she's remarked she might be open to bringing others into our games. It's a damn shame I'm too busy to approach the pirates. I think I would enjoy directing those lovely appendages all over her body.

Blast my singular focus.

I sigh quietly, slipping along the wall as the loud slurping sounds of a pretty enthusiastic blowjob echo off the tile. This is making my pussy throb and I need to keep my head on my shoulders if I'm going to get past the guards on the perimeter of the castle. What the fuck am I going to do? I duck into the next archway and suck in a deep breath as moans fill the air.

If I can't beat them...

Sending Trixie to scout the outside of the tunnel, I lean against the wall in my new hiding place. My hands come up to pinch my pierced nipples, twisting and tugging until they ache. When the sucking sound intensifies, I unzip my black cargo pants, slipping my hand into my panties. Unless I relieve this pressure, I'm going to be distracted all night and without Queenie here, this is what I'm left with.

"Jorgie..."

As the two of them murmur to each other, I circle my clit with a finger, spreading the growing wetness as it throbs. The scent of sex is permeating the enclosed area and I push two fingers inside, rocking my hips as the rusty-haired pirate whimpers and begs Jorgie for more. I'm not sure if they're in the lifestyle, but the tentacled one sounds as desperate as my girl does when I'm keeping her from her release.

Fuck, it'd be hot to top the two of them together.

That thought makes my pussy clench around my digits, and I have to bite my lip. My thumb flicks over my clit, making a shudder roll over me. I speed the motions, listening for the timing of the men and fucking myself along with their tempo. A low hissing sound is followed by a whimper and I imagine what kind of creature the punk rock Jorgie might have been to make it. Forked tongues are hot as fuck and the thought of it on me while I lick my girl to climax pushes me over the edge.

I have to control the harsh pants of my breath as the orgasm flutters through me. The exhibitionist pirates zip and gather their things, murmuring lower than I can hear. Footsteps come closer and I shrink into the darkness farther when they pause again.

"Fuck, Levi. It smells like sex and fairy dust in here. Did you sniff something before we came out of the castle?"

Oh, shit.

"Hell no, Jorgie. Even I know better than to get happy when we're on a job. I mean, happy in *that* way, not your way."

I cover my mouth, trying not to giggle. This Levi isn't stupid, but he's adorably goofy. Queenie would adore him.

"Someone must use these tunnels for an affair with a Fae. It's unmistakable... I can *taste* it."

Reptiles... those tongues are fucking astounding.

"Let's get out of here, Jorgie. We need to get the food to those people and then we can find ourselves one of the sparkling hordes to play with. They're everywhere—even this shitty ice hole."

I frown as they mention that their loot is food. Now that my brain is working, that concerns me. Trixie tugs on my pant leg and I glance down at her. She points toward the receding men and I sigh.

Looks like I'm not done with the tentacle boys yet.

"Where the hell are these douches going?" I grumble to Trixie. They lead me out of the tunnels to a serious gap in our perimeter coverage—something I'd address with that snarly yeti shifter the current queen employs as Captain of the Guard if I weren't taking mental notes on how to use it for our escape. But they're still lugging the large sacks of stolen foodstuffs and we've been walking for a long ass time.

The common villages were within a short carriage ride the last time Queenie and I did a 'goodwill tour'; why are we going so far afield?

Trixie chitters a little and I turn my attention back to the worst pirates I've ever seen as they crest the top of a tall hill. The area feels familiar—we might be on the outskirts of the kingdom where my girl chased a snow monster before I arrived. When they whistle, I sink back into the trees and hope like hell I haven't fallen into some kind of ambush. The darkly handsome Jorge scented me in the tunnels, and I could have missed some sort of communication between them.

Luckily for me, a platoon of fellow seafarers doesn't appear. Instead, a large icy bird comes soaring out of the clouds to meet them. A blue flame engulfs its body, and my jaw drops to the ground. There are legends written about this creature but most supes agree they are simply a myth—laughable considering all the species that exist, but we aren't any more exempt from irony than humans. According to the creature only forty feet from me, ice phoenixes are as real as I am.

The bird swoops down and perches on Jorge's shoulder, trilling a haunting melody. He smiles and strokes its head before he says, "Open the gates, Isa."

A flash of flame and another melody echo off the surrounding cliffs until a bright blue shield appears, then disappears. Jorge and Levi pick up their sacks, dragging them down the hill towards a large village I couldn't see before. I inch closer to the spot they were standing, dropping into the snow despite the cold. Reaching into my hip holster, I pull out the tiny metal binoculars I inherited from my time with a regency spy and peer down.

People are pouring from the houses, greeting them with cheers of thanks. Not just any people—the population of this secret town looks to be a large percentage of the commoners of the Ice Kingdom. They're all gaunt and dressed in clothes that are barely held together, but adults, children, and the elderly are crowding around the men as if they are saviors.

What in the hell is going on here? Queenie would lose her mind if she saw her people like this.

The truth hits me like a plateful of smelly trout. Queen Chelle has quietly exiled the poorest citizens of the Ice Kingdom over the years. All of her 'special' lords and ladies have taken over every inch of the viable lands and businesses until the workers and their families had nowhere to go. This town is their refugee camp and these odd thieves are playing Robin Hood to the starving people by stealing from our stores.

This is why Queenie and I got sent to the summer castle a few years ago, and it's why we aren't allowed to leave without the Queen's guards.

The phony queen of the Ice Kingdom gentrified, and she's terrified her sister—or the world at large—will find out. I can't even wrap my head around this discovery; it's so offensive that my brain won't even allow me to accept what I'm seeing. Especially because I know if I tell my girl what I found, she won't leave and I know it will be a death sentence. Without this knowledge, she was in danger, but with it, she's little more than a problem to be silenced.

What in the name of Odin am I going to do?

Scrambling to my feet, I scoop Trixie up from the branch she settled in and start the long walk back to our home with a heavy heart. I don't want to lie to Queenie now that we're on the same page. I also can't allow her soft heart to make a decision I know will lead to her demise. If we are to escape the reign of terror, her sister has imposed, I'm going to have to come up with a secondary plan to save her people on my own.

If I didn't have bad luck, I wouldn't have any luck at all.

6

GET OUT OF HERE
JACK

"I'M NERVOUS, JACKIE," QUEENIE MURMURS AS I WASH the last of the floral shampoo out of her long tresses.

She has a right to be, and that's part of why I decided we should get ready together rather than allow her handmaidens to dress her for the event. The past two weeks have been a flurry of activity—literally for her as she continued assisting the royal holiday committee with making the current queen's castle ready for the Yule ball. I, however, spent the bulk of my time working out the plans for the enormous distraction that will both allow us to escape *and* call attention to Chelle's treachery publicly that the rest of the world can't ignore. If I'm lucky, the Society may even step in to balance the scales and mete out justice, but given that Q's sister is human and so is her populace, it's unlikely.

I'll have to leave her punishment and the restructuring of the Ice Kingdom to the fairytale coalition. I don't trust them, of course, but I have few other options.

Resting my hand lightly on her waist, I brush my lips against the shell of her ear. "While you were on your best behavior with the queen's guards, I was scheming, darling. I planned for every contingency, even the unlikely ones, but I agree—we can never be sure. The only thing we know for absolute certain is we are going to get the hell out of here and not look back. Right?"

Her head bobs, but I can feel the tension in her frame. Tonight is the biggest event of the season and her sister has been prancing all over the internet, preening about her triumphs. The current queen's staff have rehearsed every single aspect of the evening from the entrance to the livestream, and our window of opportunity is quite narrow. If our distraction doesn't draw attention away from the thrones, I won't be able to whisk Queenie behind the curtains and lead her down to the tunnels where I've stashed our essential items. My plan has almost no margin for error, even with contingencies accounted for, and it's not surprising her fear of her sister's wrath has her quaking in her boots.

The contrast between this and the icy protector ready to hunt down my ex is astounding, but my girl contains multitudes, unlike her dimwitted sister.

"What if I help you relax, my love?" It's not really a question; I know what my girl needs and right now, it's focusing on something besides her fear.

"Yes, Madame," she whispers. "What is your desire?"

I swear to fuck. I'll never tire of the breathy way she says that shit. The first time made my cunt clench, and it still does years later. "On your knees."

Queenie obeys immediately, turning to face me and dropping to the river rock floor without hesitation. I grin, backing up to sit on the built-in bench of our huge wet room. This design is one of my favorites in the entire castle because of the luxurious space and fixtures. Honestly, it feels like they *made it* for situations like this and I lean back against the wall, letting the rainfall shower head cascade my body with warm water as I watch her. My thighs spread, giving her a perfect view of my pussy while she sits quietly and waits for my commands.

"Good girl," I murmur, and her skin flushes the gorgeous light pink I adore. Q mostly certainly has a praise kink and feeding it makes my body tingle in anticipation.

She rests her hands on her thighs, straightening her back so she's positioned exactly as expected, and gives me a heavy lidded expression when she replies, "Thank you, Madame."

Fuck, she's hot. How did I ever think I was leaving this behind without a thought?

"Crawl to me."

Her eyes sparkle as she moves to all fours, rolling her head in a circle to adjust her hair over the shoulders before she moves toward me slowly. My girl learned a while ago that I love when she prowls towards me like a big cat and her body moves through the water sinuously until she stops between my legs. She's back in the preferred position instantly, looking up at me through her lashes. I can tell by the way her skin is getting pinker that she's got to be dripping, but she doesn't need me to simply get her off. Queenie's anxiety will only be quelled by submitting to me before she comes, and I intend to give my love what she desperately desires.

Laying a palm on her head, I smile. "That's my girl. You may taste me as a reward."

Her face is between my thighs before I can blink and I groan darkly when an icy tongue swipes over my clit. When I glance down, her hands are gripping her own thighs tightly and I know she wants to touch me, but that's not what I gave permission for her to do. I've never been a fan of bratty submissives—those who want to top from the bottom behave like adult children and nothing about their behavior is cute or attractive. In contrast, my perfect girl tracing her tongue around my lips to lap at my juices hungrily as my body shudders? That's a thing of beauty brats can never achieve.

"You're doing such a good job, darling. I'm so pleased."

A whimper vibrates over my clit, and I press my head back against the hard rock. This is as much torture for me as it is for her, though I can certainly indulge my release whenever I choose. The emptiness inside of me is more than I can bear, though, so I reach down to yank her head up by the hair. Not hard, of course, but the semi-rough treatment has her eyes glazing over as she licks her lips.

"Yes, Madame?"

Son of a bitch.

The languid smile on my face spreads, and I growl a little. "Magical enhancements are allowed, baby. Make me come for you."

As soon as I let go, she dives back into my cunt like she's on a mission. Her tongue and teeth work over my clit until I shiver, and once I'm bucking against her soft mouth, the temperature lowers around us. Her magic swirls in the air as she creates the chilly toys I love so much. A cold, hard cock slides inside of me, contrasting with the heat of my pussy as she manipulates it to slide in and out of me slowly. I barely have time to adjust to the stretch of her icy dildo when I feel my ass stretch as well.

Queenie suckles hard on my throbbing bud, alternating the motion of her toys in rhythm with her lips.

Once you've been fucked by the Ice Queen, the bar rises to the top of Mount Olympus.

"More," I pant.

Q lifts her head for one moment, biting her lip as she smiles mischievously. A second icy assist pushes into my pussy and I gasp as the feeling of being filled to absolute maximum tips me over the edge into orgasm. My walls clench and my fingers grip the edge of the bench for purchase as I rocket through bliss. She's never done that before, and I'll be damned if it isn't blowing the top of my fucking head off. I grunt out permission for her to come—something I knew she's been holding until I give the word—and her soft, breathy moans vibrate over my sensitive flesh. It triggers another wave of pleasure and my hips arch off of the bench as I buck into her magical toys with renewed vigor.

Stars shoot in front of my eyes and I pant when I finally come down, muscles relaxing slowly. I swallow hard as Queenie's magic recedes, leaving nothing but cold water running over my heated skin. This might have been the most intense session we've ever had, and I know it's because I finally allowed her into my heart willingly. Every ounce of her submission and obedience is given out of love; it's not a means to an end.

My traitorous brain drifts to the sexy pirates I saw in the tunnels, imagining how it would look if they'd joined us in this fun. I stiffen, feeling like a complete jackass for mini-fantasy, and small hands squeeze my thighs.

"Were you not satisfied?"

Barking a laugh, I shake my head as I gesture for my girl to rise from the floor. "Queenie, my love, you were perfect. My darling good girl did exactly as she was told, and now it's time for me to take care of you." Her smile is bright as I force myself to stand on wobbly legs, gathering the cloth and soap to wash us clean again as I hold her. "When you're clean and relaxed, I'll dry us and we will cuddle on the bed until it's time to finish getting dressed."

The look on her face makes my heart squeeze and I wing a prayer to gods I don't believe in that I've created a scheme that will allow me to take care of her for the rest of our immortal lifespans.

As I FINISH the intricate braid, I smile at my girl in the mirror. I keep my hair cropped short for a multitude of reasons, but the biggest is that I could never sit still like this and have someone tug and pull at it for formal styles. They have taught Queenie to endure this since she was a wee princess, so she's happily reading while I spray, twist, and decorate her. She looks up and chats with me occasionally, then stops when she instinctively knows I'm focusing. It's eerie how well she can read my moods, to be honest.

I suppose if you've lived with a mercurial narcissist for most of your life, you become an expert in when to make yourself small.

"There. Perfect. You look beautiful." I study her reflection in the mirror for a moment and pause. "Before we go in, add some magical snowflakes and sparkle to complement the necklace."

Once again, I'm dressed in matching shades of blue and white to complement her glittering white Yule gown. This time, however, I helped her accessorize under the large skirt to facilitate our plan. Q has my pants from the last party rather than bloomers and we stitched tear away velcro at the waistline. When we sneak off during the distraction, we'll dispose of the skirt and use the thick coats we stowed to cover her bare shoulders and arms. It's a hike to the first hideout, and I have to make sure she's dressed for the weather.

"You made certain all of our disguises and things were still hidden earlier?" she asks. "My hair will give us away if anyone spots us before we make it to the border."

"I did it while you were applying your war paint, love. Everything is ready, I promise."

"Trixie knows what to do?"

My mischievous companion lets out her signature noise, pumping a small fist like she's cheering, and we both laugh. "I think that's a 'yes', darling."

Queenie is nervous as hell despite our session. It's not only the worry about her sister catching us—it's fear of the unknown. She's rarely been out of the Ice Kingdom and before they hired me, she had no access to the internet. They limited her knowledge of the outside world to what I've shared with her and vague memories from childhood. My girl had no idea what to expect because she's been basically held prisoner most of her life.

There's so much we're going to do and see once we get free; I can't wait to show it to her.

"Good." She lifts her chin and looks at me, her eyes serious. "I'm ready to find out what the rest of our lives look like."

Hell yes, baby.

51

7

BACKSTABBER
QUEENIE

THE PALACE IS HUMMING WITH ACTIVITY WHEN WE arrive.

Jalokiviä, the drooling hairy yeti shifter my sister made captain of her guard, is waiting for us in the livery. He's short and squat for his kind, with an unearned air of importance and questionable hygiene. His association with the queen gives him carte blanche to act as though he's important, and that's why he's glaring at Jackie and I imperiously. His eyes skim over us with disgustingly obvious intent and he licks his lips salaciously.

Someone as repugnant and dim-witted as Jalokiviä has as much chance of attracting women like us as he does completing a Times Sunday crossword—zero.

Jackie clears her throat, giving me an amused expression, and I realize I fixed my face in an uncharacteristic sneer. I've never questioned or responded to how most of the castle staff treat me, but I also didn't know my sister sanctioned their contempt. The way they behave can only result from Bella weaving lies and half-truths to make herself seem appealing, and me look like a monster. Having seen my past through clear eyes, I cannot go back to pretending the current queen is the persona she's crafted so carefully.

"You two will enter through the staff tunnels. Her Majesty will have you inspected before you may enter areas not relegated to servants. I will escort you to ensure you cannot do anything that will embarrass Her Highness during this important holiday celebration," the yeti says in a flat tone.

I arch a brow and open my mouth, but Jackie is the one who steps forward. "Jalokiviä, you should be proud! You recited an entire script full of words with more than one syllable and your brain didn't leak out of your nostrils. It truly is a Yule miracle!"

Coughing to hide my snicker, I gaze at him with wide eyes. Men, even shifters, will always choose to believe women are clueless if presented with the right visual cues. "Oh, Jackie, you're so funny! The Captain will be a wonderful companion to us while we wait for the queen's assistant to give us a once over."

He looks at us suspiciously, but finally nods. "Go sit on the benches over there. Mikkeline will be here shortly."

Jackie rolls her eyes before walking me over to the benches outside of the main staff prep area. I can feel her disdain for the oafish lout who has been serving my family since I was a girl. "Traitorous fool," she hisses under her breath as we sit. "He and the elders who allowed your sister to isolate and ostracize you based on nothing more than her word deserve to be tied to the mountain and left for the eagles to feast on."

I believe she'd do it if we were staying.

Since our talk, Jackie's anger at the people who orchestrated my eventual surrender of my throne has only increased. I've tried to help her see that fear and self-preservation were likely the reasons no one ever questioned Bella, but she refuses to accept it. In her mind, anyone who knew and stayed quiet or simply chose not to see us as guilty as anyone who was complicit. She looked me dead in the eye and quoted a *human,* of all things.

"The only thing necessary for evil to triumph in the world is for good men to do nothing, Queenie. Someday, they'll all pay for their cowardice."

I had to look it up on her phone—I've never been allowed much access to the real world—but a man named Edmund Burke was supposed to have said it, but that was proven false. The trail I followed led to a similar attribution by John Stuart Mill, and he believed in social reform. Since we're trapped in a monarchy where the queen has gone quite mad, I understood why she'd say it. The Ice Kingdom desperately needs a leader who is not so power hungry that she'd abuse her own family in the name of fame and money.

But I doubt we'll ever return to right the wrongs—once I leave, we will have to stay hidden forever or I'm certain Bella will use every weapon she has to extort our return. Her political sway is quite far-reaching. Since we've been exporting the pure glacier water from our land, that pressure could easily sway politicians around the globe.

My presence has been required in diplomatic functions for years and I pay attention despite the prevailing opinion that I'm merely a pretty set piece.

"We only need to get through tonight, love. After that, the Ice Kingdom will have to fend for itself." A flash of guilt crosses her face and I lean in to whisper in her ear. "The people will eventually rise against my sister if she continues her nasty ways. They outnumber her greatly, even with her guards and rich friends."

"I'm sure they will," she murmurs as she looks at her hands. "That's a tale as old as time."

Chuckling softly, I bump her shoulder with mine. "That line belongs to another of my Princess brethren. You're in the wrong fairy tale."

Her smile is fleeting, but she wraps an arm around me and squeezes me to her side. "True. Do you remember the protocols we went over?"

My eyes dart to Jalokiviä and I nod, choosing my response carefully. "I do. Everything before the procession and after the lighting of the candles."

"Good," she replies. "It's imperative we follow the steps to the letter or there will be consequences."

The yeti snorts, letting me know she was right to be cautious of his hearing. He may not have caught our low tones, but our normal voices carried enough for him to eavesdrop. "I'm well aware of what will happen if we do not follow protocol."

The last time I misbehaved, I paid the price and I won't have it happen again.

"Jacqueline! Elle!"

Our conversation halts as the blond woman dressed in a svelte, sparkling power suit claps her hands at us like we're dogs. Mikkeline gives us a wide, phony smile as she waits for us to come to her. Jalokiviä laughs under his breath, clearly enjoying a lowly staffer treating me as if I'm a peasant. I stand, schooling

56

my face into the cool glare of a royal before offering my hand to Jackie. She takes it and joins me, gripping my palm to calm me.

"How kind of you to make time for us on this important evening, Mikkeline. My sister is so gracious to lend her assistant to us."

The haughty woman looks down her nose at me, sniffing before she replies. "The Queen asked me to verify you wouldn't be an embarrassment to her at this auspicious occasion because I am her most trusted confidant. Do not mistake it for a favor, Elle; it is a statement of how little you matter."

The gall of this glorified office manager is unmatched, but I cannot let her see my fury. Only small people take pleasure in tearing others down for their own personal fulfillment.

"I suggest you do your job and scurry off to put your nose back in the crack it lives in, Mikkeline. It wouldn't do for the entire staff to see you showing your true colors," Jack says with a bored look on her face. "I mean, it's common knowledge you're a yipping lap dog who is paid less than an intern—it'd be a shame if they all realize you're also doing the queen's dirty work."

My lips curve briefly and I simply look at the parasitic assistant my sister chose because of her willingness to sacrifice her morals for a brush with fame. She stares back for a few moments before stepping back to examine our outfits and nods, furiously typing something into her phone. The Captain rolls his eyes, clearly less of a fan of the asskissing bitch than we are.

"You aren't good enough for the procession—as usual—because I have already invited the Queen's loyal fans, but you may attend as you are. However, if you step one foot out of line at my party, I'll have you escorted out immediately."

Of course, she considers planning a party for my sister and the other nobles as her invitation to the elite. This woman was only a bored homemaker a year ago, but now she fancies herself a powerbroker because my sister and her ilk allowed her to soak up some of their spotlight by being in their presence. Whether she's good at what she does or not, she's no more part of their world than I am, but here she is, looking down her nose at me.

Pathetic.

"Understood. We have no desire to take part in your ridiculous parade of privilege and nepotism, anyway. Queenie doesn't need it to establish her identity—unlike the people you serve." My girl crosses her arms over her chest, giving the assistant a sickly sweet smile as she shoos her. "Go reapply the brown to your nose and leave us in peace."

The huff Mikkeline leaves in makes Jalokiviä snort, but I don't react. He may not like her, but he won't take our side if this comes to a confrontation with Bella. The staff here are aware their livelihoods depend on the whims of the queen, and even if he is a tool, I wouldn't want to put his position in jeopardy. I'm a far better person than the people who allowed her to exile me to the woods like a monster without proof.

"And now we wait," I murmur.

"Indeed. The game is afoot," Jackie whispers in my ear as we settle on the bench again.

Hopefully, our psychotic nemesis doesn't drag us over a waterfall like Mr. Holmes.

Fairy lights glitter in the throne room as soft music plays and the lords and ladies mingle. An enormous spread of food is laid out on one side of the room and servants glide through the crowd with drinks and appetizers as groups chatter animatedly. One would never know the evil that lurks under this layer of shining elegance—every inch of the image is curated so the livestream appears perfect. They filled even the impeccably decorated tree and garlands with the results of my magic to help create a Winter Wonderland.

It makes me sick to know I had to play a role in making my sister look like a generous and beneficent leader.

But I've been doing it for a long time—I stood by her side and crowed about her accomplishments in public as directed, despite her lack of reciprocal respect or support. I didn't have a choice; Bella is my sister, and I willingly allowed her to usurp my identity to glorify herself. If I'd seen her true face sooner, perhaps I wouldn't be forced to stay in the shadows as she flits about extolling her virtues to the world. My inability to see the glaring red flags in our relationship has made it impossible to expose the real queen in public without risking my freedom.

"Stop beating yourself up, Q. You didn't know."

Sighing, I glance at Jackie, then turn my eyes back to the doorway where the processional will enter momentarily. We can't be seen as ignoring the Queen's big entrance so I can't face her for long. "I didn't, but because of my naïveté, others are suffering and will continue to suffer after I'm gone. Knowing that I helped her ascend this throne of false notoriety is a tough pill to swallow. Without my vocal support, she would have remained a small-time royal with a kingdom who didn't recognize her rule."

"That's true. Her personality would have been harder to disguise without the enthusiastic approval you gave her, but everyone makes mistakes with people they care about. Fuck knows, my cock-ups are well documented in the media. Take your own advice and let it go, Elle."

I see what she did there. When she first arrived, all I did was encourage her to let go of her past through song and it drove her insane.

"Hilarious, Jackie. But I see your point. I can't control what the rest of the world does, even when I know they're buying a load of horseshit. They have choices like I did."

Her arms wrap around my waist and she sits her chin on my shoulder as the music stops abruptly and the sounds of the heralds fill the air. My sister never appears in public without a protracted introduction designed to lord her 'success' and power over everyone present. The Yule celebration will not be an exception. Every public appearance and event is about her in her mind and she can't help but act as though the entire world is waiting for her with bated breath.

I watch as the members of her band of toadies and brown nosers glide by, waving and nodding at the crowd like their proximity to the queen makes them better than they are. On their own, they are little more than tiny fish in a sea of merchants and artisans. Despite that, they act as though they are at the top of the food chain.

When I ruled the Ice Kingdom, I did away with most of this nonsense purposefully. Every citizen has an important contribution to our ecosystem and these sullen twits don't need the ego boost of being lauded like they work nearly as hard as the rest of my people. My sister was all for equality and giving everyone the recognition they deserved until she clawed her way to the throne. Now she preaches acceptance in public and privately denigrates everyone who doesn't worship her like a snake in the tall weeds.

I should have known how she'd behave by the way she spent much of our 'sister bonding' time gossiping about the more successful monarchs and kingdoms.

Bella was convinced they were out to make her look bad or conniving to steal from our kingdom. She pretended to admire the more powerful or wealthy kings and queens abroad, but when the cameras turned off, her harsh words revealed her jealousy. I'm ashamed to admit, even to myself, that I took part in her nasty rants because I was simply ecstatic she was including me. When her paranoia reached its peak, I pulled away, and that's when I was exiled. Eventually, she burned the Enchanted Forest to the ground because I disagreed with her and wouldn't relent. That should have been the moment I saw her for who she really was, but I didn't. I was too afraid of the iron grip she'd cultivated on our people and the rest of the world.

I knew she could sway them to attack and possibly destroy me if she felt like it and if I made a stand, she definitely would.

"Here she comes," Jackie whispers in my ear. Her words make my spine straighten and I refocus on the double doors as I wait for Bella to enter.

The trumpets blare, and the orchestra plays the opening notes of her famous theme song, filling the air with the sweet notes of a love song that no longer applies. Ornate doors fly open and Bella stands in between them, with Mikkeline and Jalokiviä a step behind her. Despite the holidays, she's dressed in a long black dress with a mermaid tail held up by her ladies-in-waiting and they piled her red hair on top of her head. I blink when I see how sallow her skin looks and evidence of dark circles under her eyes despite the legions of makeup artists who no doubt had her in their chairs before dawn today.

Once she's certain everyone's eyes are on her, my sister strides into the room with her fake smile plastered on her countenance like a mask. Her head tilts as she gives her acolytes subtle smirks when she passes them until she finally alights the steps to the obnoxiously bejeweled throne she erected for herself when she took over. Servants rush to assist her with positioning the ridiculous dress in the perfect position for the cameras, and I roll my eyes internally. Her ego has grown so enormous; I'm surprised she can even fit in the seat with it on board. This is the epitome of being a dilettante, and it reeks of the 'phony king of England' style nonsense.

Jackie chuckles as my energy shifts to disgust, and she squeezes me. "Don't let her bullshit affect you, darling. I know it irks you to see her behaving like this, but we have to maintain our calm. We'll be far away from this, eventually."

I nod, concentrating on evening out my breaths as my sister addresses the crowd in her usual imperious fashion. Her speech is full of vague insults and barbs that will only be recognized by those 'in the know' about her various enemies and nemeses—including me. Jackie tenses up every time she hears a potshot at me, but I pat her hand reassuringly. Bella has been doing this to me for a long time and though I didn't understand, she was purposely crushing my ego to keep me in line. Her slights and hissy fits—both public and private—were designed to prevent me from stepping out of her shadow because she couldn't compete.

Lucky for her, I have no interest in stealing her minions. I'm headed for sunnier climes where I'm not shackled to a self-centered egomaniac.

My sister finally ends her typical rambling bout of emotional masturbation with hat tips to her cultish followers in the front rows and I let out a sigh of relief. Now that she's shut up, the guests will eat and do their typical underhanded rich people's shady business shit until it's time to light the candles. Once we get to that ceremony, Jackie and I execute our plan.

After that, I'll be on the run until we get to the last stop, but then...*freedom.*

There's no revenge sweeter than breaking the chains of oppression and leaving behind your abuser.

8

THE ATTACK ON THE HOUSE
LEVI

"Tell me again why we came to this dog and pony show?"

Jorgie sighs as if I'm the most infuriating being on the planet. It's not the first time he's looked at me that way and it won't be the last. I have zero patience for all the foppery of shit like this and he knows it. I'd much rather be raiding the coffers or partying with normal people. There's not a supe in this room—outside of staff—who has the slightest idea what it means to work for anything. It makes my skin crawl to saunter around and make inane conversation with the elites we target with our schemes and scams.

"Levi, we have to use our connections to find the ripest plums in the orchard. Attending fancy parties and celebrations is our best source of intel. Without the information we gather here, we won't be able to continue helping the people who need us," he murmurs.

Of course, he's right; he's always right. Jorgie is all logic and I'm all heart, which is why we make such an efficient team.

"It reminds me of home and I hate it. The best decision I ever made was abdicating my birthright and letting my idiot brother take the throne. Now I'm free to sail around with you and actually make a difference." I tug on the collar of the stiff neck of my dress shirt with a growl of frustration. Being bound up in this formal nonsense doesn't help with my mood, either. I have to make certain I don't shift or I'll rip everything—that will only draw unwanted attention.

My boyfriend gives me a knowing look. "Keep your temper in check, big guy. You know, part of the agreement with Triton was that you would ensure that you didn't embarrass your family in public. That was the stipulation he demanded in exchange for not declaring you exiled."

"Yes, yes. I have to keep my tentacles to myself or I'll be cut off. I'm well aware. That asshole knows how uncomfortable it is to stay in my humanoid form for long periods of time—he included that clause on purpose. His petty revenge for having to horse trade for a throne he believed our father should have given to him." Running my hand through my hair, I clench my fists at my side in frustration. To this day, that clause never ceases to infuriate me.

"Did you see Queen Bella enter? That had to be the most ostentatious procession I've ever seen for a kingdom this small. She strutted down the aisle as if she ruled Valhalla. Most amusing." Jorgie jerks his head in the ruler's direction in question as she perches on her tacky throne. "This event and the accouterments of her castle are why her people are clumped in a camp on the outskirts of the capital. She's created her own illusion of grandeur in the center of the kingdom, so outsiders don't watch closely at what's really going on here."

Squinting at the dais, I watch as the queen's sister and her companion quietly slip out from behind the curtains and take their seat on a lower level. The two women are clearly being as obsequious as possible, so they draw any eyes away from Queen Bella and I'm certain that's by design. Triton never wanted me around when he was holding court, and when I grew tired of his idiotic machinations, Jorgie and I set sail for adventure. Both women are stunning in diametrically opposite ways—the former queen has flowing hair and soft curves, while her companion is tall and solidly built with an adorable pixie cut. I watch the way they interact for a moment, then elbow my companion.

"The former queen and her attendant are a couple. They look at each other the way we do." My eyes dance as I gesture to the royals in icy blue and white. "And I think neither of them is human. Something about the way they move exudes barely contained power."

"Hmmm," Jorgie says as he tilts his head. "Perhaps that's our way into more than the stores of the Summer Palace. Queen Elle seems nervous; her eyes are darting around the room as if she's watching for something, and her companion has the look of a woman with vast experience. Do we know who she is?"

Pulling out my phone, I do a quick internet search. It takes less than a minute to identify the woman who appears to be comforting the tremulous ex-queen. "Oh, fuck, J! That's Jack... *the* Jack. You know, from like... everything. Before this, she was the one on that web show with the chick who died. They both fell off the balcony during some big party?"

"We need to monitor them, Levi. It's fairly common knowledge Jack has gotten a raw deal from her former employers and she could be a valuable ally. I doubt she has a love for the current Queen even if she is involved with her sister. She may help us transfer some of this obnoxious wealth back to the people of the Ice Kingdom before we move on.

I grin. Schmoozing people is my job and planning is his—that means I'll get close to Jack and her girl. I'm all for it because they are both smoking hot. If I get lucky, I'll wangle an invitation to guest star in their bedroom olympics. Group activities are my favorite and Jorgie *loves* to watch before he joins. "Aye, aye, Captain!"

"Odin, save me. You're never going to let go of the pirate shit, are you?" He scrubs a hand down his face and gives me a pleading look.

"Hell no! I'm a son of the sea, sailing the seas, and stealing from the rich assholes who live near it. Pirates, we will always be!" I pause for a moment and give him a crooked grin. "Besides, we're headed for the Caribbean next, and you know how much I love that human movie. I can't wait to bitch about the rum being gone!"

Jorgie gives me a dark look. His gaze narrows as he reaches over to swat my ass. "Behave, Levi. We have loot to locate and then we need to pull up anchor. We've already been here longer than I'm comfortable with."

I open my mouth to retort, but another loud blast comes from the heralds on the stage. The crowd goes silent as they watch the Queen rise from her ridiculous perch and smile like a cat that got the cream.

"Friends, citizens, and honored guests... it's time to begin the Yulemas ceremony."

Well, shit. I don't know what fresh hell this is, but it's going to keep us from slipping through the crowd unnoticed.

I'VE BEEN to quite a few winter celebrations in my time, but this one feels unnecessarily drawn out.

The Ice Kingdom isn't very different from the other Norse-type kingdoms Jorgie and I have been to, but Queen Bella seems determined to preside over the most extravagant shit I've ever seen. They've lit candles all over the room, carved runes into the Yule log, decorated a Yulemas tree, and now she's giving her third lengthy speech. They have preceded each tradition with one and even her loyalists look bored. She needs to light the damn wreath on fire and toss it; no one has consumed enough alcohol to suffer through this for much longer.

"And now I will light the Yule wreath so we may burn it as a prayer for the return of the Sun!"

Thank fuck.

"Levi!"

I frown, looking over at Jorgie as he beckons for me to step back from the crowd in front of us. "What? If I had to listen to that shit, I want to see the fire."

"The former queen and her companion surreptitiously moved from their seats to behind the curtain. Can you think of a reason they would risk the ire of their monarch during her moment of glory?" Jorgie arches his brow and looks around. "Something isn't right. Follow me."

His powers don't include premonition, but he has uncanny senses when it comes to danger. I don't know if it's the scent changing in the room or something in his immortal DNA, but Jorgie is rarely wrong about this sort of thing. I nod and he wraps his hand around my wrist—that's when I realize he's anxious. The super strength combined with the feel of his scales forming over his skin tells me whatever he's feeling is making him paranoid as hell. Jorgie has to be extremely careful with allowing his powers to surface. He has the power to plunge the world into a dystopian nightmare if he's not careful.

We all have our quirks, right? I think it's hot as fuck that he's a harbinger of doom.

Weaving our way through the crowd towards the exit the beautiful ladies took, I look over my shoulder at the fiery spinning Yule wreath. Before we duck into the door they must have taken, a minor explosion propels the tiny flames on the traditional circle of fir. The crowd gasps in shock and after that, it's like everything moves in slow motion. The fire leaps to an invisible line on the floor, traveling straight to the tree; it bursts into enormous flames immediately.

That's when the screaming starts.

"Stop fucking around, Levi! We have to get out of here before the fire spreads or the smoke... or hell, the goddamn guards start trampling people to get to their ruler!"

I duck into the concealed door with Jorgie, my eyes wide as we descend a pitch black stairway. Something small and furry brushes my leg and I yelp. "Hades in a sex swing, was that an enormous rat?!"

"Shhh!" His hand tightens on my arm and I close my mouth as he guides us through the darkness. His voice is a low whisper when we reach the bottom of the winding steps. "I don't know where we're going, but it smells like we're in the tunnels. A different part than the other night, perhaps, but I'm sure we will eventually hit the lighted portion."

"I'm more concerned about giant plague rats than electricity," I mutter. Jorgie has excellent night vision, so I know he's capable of keeping us from being discovered, but I'd like to exit this cold ass castle without a virulent disease. I'm fond of my body parts exactly in the condition they arrived in.

A soft laugh startles me. "Levi, are you obsessing about the rats and germs?"

"Of course I am!" I huff. "Laugh all you want about my fancy airs, but good hygiene is essential to a long life."

"I'm immortal, you dipstick."

"Good thing one of us is. My golden sheen left the building like Elvis when I gave up my throne to gallivant around the world with *you*." If he could see my sneer, I'm sure I'd get a delightful spanking, but as it is, he's too busy scenting our way through the maze under this massive iceberg. The tunnels are winding and confusing—I'm surprised they don't have a fucking Minotaur down here freezing his furry balls off.

"Huh."

"You're going to have to give me more than that, Jorgie. It's pitch black in here and I can't even read your expression. I have no idea why you're making your 'a-ha' sound." I roll my eyes as he stops our progress and goes still. I know better than to speak

71

until he answers—I'd wager he's holding his free hand to lips to shush me, though I can't see it.

"I smell... magic. Earthy, flowery forest magic with hints of cold frost and hints of the ocean. It's close," he whispers.

"For the love of... *illuminate*!"

My eyes widen as the sound of a voice like bourbon and honey echoes through the cave, followed by a loud clap. Tiny fairy lights embedded in the tunnel walls blink on, casting shadows on the women standing in front of Jorgie and I. The short-haired companion is holding a wicked looking short sword, crackling with the magic that is lighting up the room. Elle, the former queen of the Ice Kingdom, is glaring at us through electric blue eyes while holding a swirling ball of snowflakes in her palm. When neither of us speaks up, they look at one another, communicating without words before turning back.

"*Who. The Fuck. Are. You?*" The infamous Jack doesn't mince words, apparently.

Jorgie lets go of my wrist and steps forward to bow at the waist. "Your Highness. Levi and I are honored to meet you, even under these inauspicious circumstances. Apologies for frightening you and your companion."

A trill of laughter makes me look at them all in confusion, and the Snow Queen turns to Jack with a smile. "What an odd man. You spoke to him, yet he addressed me. I'm not a ventriloquist."

Jack shakes her head, not lowering the sword as she nods. "Indeed, Queenie. These gentlemen are desperately trying to distract us from asking why they are in our private tunnels. I assume they will assert they found the door and thought to escape the fire upstairs and simply happened upon us. However,

I know for a fact they were in the tunnels below *our* castle the last time I toured them. Therefore, they must have nefarious intentions."

Holy fuck, she was there that night?

My lips curve into a lecherous grin as I wonder exactly what the snub nosed swords woman witnessed. I certainly enjoyed the tête-à-tête; I can only hope she saw something she liked as well. Both of them are even more attractive brandishing weapons than they were posing on a stage, and I like my ladies to have a little spice with their sugar.

"Down, boy," Jorgie mutters as his forked tongue flicks out.

Damn. He never *loses control like that. These girls are affecting him, too.*

"Your companion caught us, Queen Elle. We were in the tunnels below your palace earlier in the month and we have been in these tunnels before as well. Not this section, but..." I smile and shrug, deciding to take a chance. "They hired us to assist some of your villages with gathering information about the goings-on in the castle and we are merely good hearted rogues. We mean you no harm."

"Spies, huh?" Jack drawls as she looks from one of us to the other. I don't know if she saw our spoils or even if she followed us to the resistance village, so I wait for her to continue. "I'm no fan of such intrigue, but it's possible we can work out a mutually beneficial arrangement."

Is she blackmailing us in front of her girl? Fuck, this chick is the absolute tits.

"Go on," Jorgie says. "But tell us with your weapons sheathed."

"Party pooper," the ex-queen grumbles as her snowflakes fade and the aura around her goes back to normal. "I don't get to play with my magic much. I was looking forward to freezing their dicks off, Jackie."

Another low, husky laugh escapes her lips as she sheaths her sword and ruffles the queen's hair fondly. "I know, darling. Perhaps if they piss us off again, you'll get your chance." The warrior turns back to us, folding her arms over her chest. "You need us to keep our mouths shut about your... spying... and we need a ride."

"A ride?" I snort. "There are at least twenty carriages in this place!"

Snowflakes fly into the air as the Snow Queen shakes her head. "You misunderstand, gentlemen. We are not looking to hitch-hike to another place in the Ice Kingdom. We're leaving and we need you to ferry us as far out of the reach of my sister as possible."

Jack grins as she puts her hands on her hip. "This isn't a heist; it's a jailbreak."

Holy fucking banana pants... did we get conscripted to save a princess?

9

RUN AWAY WITH ME
JACK

To their credit, Jorgie and Levi don't freak out. I would not have been surprised if they did—we're asking them to be branded as kidnappers and commit treason at worst. Queen Bella doesn't have a lot of allies, but she is gifted at playing the victim on camera. She'll no doubt milk our disappearance for every ounce of sympathy she can get to dominate the news cycle.

There's nothing a covert narcissist like her loves more than soaking up the spotlight with their tales of woe.

"Perhaps... we are misunderstanding what you want, Queen Elle," Jorgie starts.

Queenie cuts him off with a firm shake of her head. "Impossible. I was very blunt and neither of you seem stupid. We want you to smuggle us out of the Ice Kingdom, preferably to a sunny island south of the equator."

"But Your Majesty..."

This time, I roll my eyes. "Levi, she didn't stutter. Also, she hates being called those things. Elle will be fine."

They stare at one another, communicating silently. It seems to be a battle of wills expressed through eyebrows and scowls until finally the tentacled redhead beams. He turns back to us with a suspiciously excited expression.

"Jorgie is unsure, but I like the cut of your jib, ladies. However, what you're asking of us carries a punishment far worse than being caught stealing. Are you open to negotiating your price?"

Pirates... no matter the species, they only have their minds on the booty. Which booty depends on the day, but they're wholly predictable.

"We are, but this will have to be discussed in a less treacherous location, boys. Our distraction upstairs won't hold for much longer and we're wasting getaway time," I reply. I squint into the darkness and let out a low whistle, smiling when Trixie scrambles out of the shadows to join us.

"Holy shit, he wasn't kidding about the fucking rat." Jorgie eyes the capuchin on my shoulder and I have to smother a giggle when she flips him off with her tiny monkey hands.

I taught her that and look at how useful it was.

"Trixie is clearly a monkey, not a rat, and Jackie is right. We're going to get caught if we don't haul ass to our things and run like hell from this place." Queenie puts her hands on her hips and glares at them both like they're recalcitrant children.

"Fine!" Levi grumbles. "But if either of you have a trunk with an industrial strength hair dryer, I'm out."

My girl looks confused, but I give them a withering look at the reference. As if I'd try to transport huge beauty supplies when Q and I were planning on stealing horses to lead through the Black Forest. The very idea is insulting.

"We packed extremely lightly so we can move quickly, you jackass. Tuck your misogyny in before I let Queenie freeze your boys off like she wanted earlier." My smirk is playful, but my eyes say I'm not joking, so they nod.

Threatening their dicks is the oldest and most effective way to control a man, even if they have tentacles and snake tongues.

The four of us trudge through the caves I mapped out, following the glowing sigils I scribbled on the walls. It doesn't take long to reach the hidden compartment I stowed our packs in and I sling mine over my shoulders before gesturing to Queenie. She spins around and I tug on the tear away section of the poofy dress, peeling the heavy skirts off. The boys stand there gaping at us like fools as I stuff the material in the hole and hand her the pack with her shit in it.

"What?" Queenies demand as they continue to stare. "Did you think because we're women or I was a queen that we don't have common sense? Good lord, this is going to be a long trip if you don't trust Jackie to make plans. She's a brilliant strategist—who do you think plotted all those silly web shows?"

"*You* wrote the *Jack & Jill* show?!" Levi gasps as if I've revealed a state secret. "You? Not Jill?"

Huffing, I walk over to tighten Queenie's straps and then face them both. "Most of them. Jill wasn't keen on admitting that, so I let her take the spotlight. It was a mistake and only fed her ego until the eventual tragedy. Now, can we move on?"

Jorgie tilts his head, studying me for a moment. He opens his mouth and shuts it, obviously deciding forcing me to rehash my former life is best left to another time. That would be never if I had my way and I'll make sure it never comes up again if I can help it. Talking about the abuse I suffered at Jill's hands before her meltdown is embarrassing and infuriating, so anything I can do to avoid it is fair game.

"Okay, but I'm gonna want to talk about that later," Levi grumbles. "I *knew* the last season felt like it went off the rails."

He has no *idea.*

"We need to go this way," I announce. "This tunnel will let out near the stables and I've made certain two fine horses will be ready for us. They aren't our usual mounts because it would be obvious, but I've also been leaving clues all over the castle and tunnels that will hopefully lead the moronic guards to believe someone has actually kidnapped us. It will slow down their search for a while."

Queenie takes my arm and follows me, but I can hear Levi muttering to Jorgie in the background. "That's not a strategy; it's the plot to the *Princess Bride*. They better have more on tap than that, or we'll dangle by dawn."

"I *heard that*!" I hiss.

Of course, neither of them needed to know I only had three weeks to amend my original plan to get the hell out of Dodge because I took my girl with me. My commitment trauma is none of their goddamn business and I don't owe them an explanation. They're tagging along on *my* plan and they can bite me if they don't like it.

Which, honestly, I might like, but that is also none of their business.

"OKAY, if either of you comment on the fucking horses I chose, I'm getting my soprano maker out," I grumble as we make our way through the dark stables.

I wasn't worried about Queenie when I picked the two fastest horses, but she doesn't have the pop culture knowledge these dipshits do. Queen Bella kept her shit in like Kimmy Schmidt and the only things she knows are what I've watched with her over the years. I specifically avoided the movie Levi mentioned because it was a favorite of one of my exes and well... they better keep their big mouths closed or I'm gonna create a few *castrati*.

"Aye, aye, milady," Levi says cheerfully. "I can't call you Captain because it'd be weird."

"Considering she dated that dope, it sure would!"

I whirl around, giving Queenie a death stare. That was yet another piece of my history I didn't need shared with Heckle & Jeckle over there. They'll never let it go and—

"No way!"

Jorgie grimaces and sighs. "Sweet baby Thor, woman. Are you a storybook groupie? He's going to ram this down our throats for the entire ride. Not to mention the amount of questions you're going to get on the long fucking sea voyage about your illustrious bedposts."

"Aw, Jorgie, don't be jealous! I love all your crazy stories, too. And your dick is huge. It's a big bonus."

Queenie's mouth drops open and I throw my back in laughter. These two are the grumpiest and sunshiniest assholes I've ever met, and I have no idea how they put up with one another, but it's endearing. We could have found *much* worse companions to undertake months of sailing with. That's not to say I may not murder Levi before we make land, but at least I'll get a few chuckles out of it.

"You've got a dirty mouth, Levi. I can't decide if I like it or not."

The sea shifter shrugs and winks at my girl. "That's because you haven't had it on you yet. Trust me, it won't be a hard decision," he practically purrs.

She gives him a look that's part indignant and part interested, but ultimately, she stomps on his foot and stalks to the end of the row of horses in a huff. Both of the guys arch a brow at me, and I shrug before I follow her.

Yup, the Ice Queen and I are going to have to have a little chat.

"Oh, Jackie, you picked Buttercup and Wesley!" She squeals in delight, and the muffled snorts behind me make my spine stiffen in irritation.

When they approach with bemused expressions, I tap the hilt of my sword and they sober immediately. "Yes, I did. They are two of the fastest horses in this stable, and neither of us rides them often. I'm going to leave a few things in one of their stalls to throw off the guards, but we won't be able to take any others. We'll have to double up."

"Who's riding with who? Obviously, based on weight, you ladies won't be able to ride together because we're too big to ride together for this long of a journey." Jorgie holds back as he asks us, eyeing the horse warily while Levi approaches them excitedly.

80

Queenie strokes Buttercup's muzzle as she looks at the men. "By size, I believe Levi and I should ride Buttercup, and you should take Wesley. That will distribute the size fairly equally."

"Don't worry, Elle! I'm aces with equines. My father created them and some of my brothers are horses," Levi boasts as he ruffles the mane of the chestnut colored mare.

My brows furrow, and I tilt my head. "Is your father... Poseidon, Levi?"

"Duh," he says as he leads Buttercup out of the stall.

"My brother is a horse, too," Jorgie grumbles. He gives the kraken a dirty look as he waits for us to get the animals ready. "Showoff."

I blink, still processing that information, and Queenie pinches my arm. "It's very impressive and I'm sure his dark companion is equally endowed with glory, but we must go, love."

My girl definitely doesn't get why I'm impressed, but she isn't wrong. "We'll discuss this later. Jorgie, get your gloomy ass over here and ride with me. We need to put some miles between us and the people who will hunt us."

Hopping on the black horse, I watch Levi help Queenie mount Buttercup. He takes her pack and puts it on, then climbs behind her with a big grin. I'm going to have to watch him—he's a huge flirt and Q has been so sheltered that she doesn't realize what he's blatantly suggesting.

"You don't have to worry about him."

The voice in my ear makes me shriek and I turn to glare at the broody pirate. "A little warning would be nice. You could get punched in the junk if you're not careful."

"What is your obsession with our dicks? It's weird considering what you... witnessed... the other night," Jorgie rumbles. He hasn't moved away from my ear and his breath skates over my skin.

Somehow, I don't think the golden retriever is the one I need to worry about.

Looking over my shoulder, I shrug. "Voyeurism is very chic at the moment. You should consider that for next time."

That said, I click the reins and start guiding Wesley out into the paddock. I hear Queenie's horse following and I let out a sigh of relief.

I have no idea what this journey is going to look like, but anything is better than letting Queen Bella take away the shine my girl has exuded since we left the throne room. Hands tighten on my waist and I raise my chin. Jorgie and Levi are going to help us leave the Ice Kingdom and my girl will never be suppressed again.

I'll kill anyone who dares to try.

10

VIOLENT DELIGHTS

JORGIE

I'M NOT FOND OF LAST-MINUTE CHANGES AND LEVI knows it.

I wrap my hands around the woman he called Jack, holding on as we gallop across the countryside in the dead of night. Levi acted as though I should know who she is, but he often forgets that I'm not a rabid consumer of media unless he watches with me. I prefer a good book by far and I enjoy reading to him even more. But he's the first being in many millennia to interest me enough to stick around, so I indulge his whims more than I should.

The restless spirit comes from my unpredictable father and his endless quest to torment the rest of our family.

Shaking my head so my hair catches the wind and moves out of my eyes, I study my riding companion. She's sturdily built, and I'd wager she has at least a touch of Fae in her, based on the pointed ears. I gathered that her immortality was sealed by her fairy tale status from Levi's gushing, so I'm not concerned by the breakneck pace she has our mount pushing. It's obvious she's well practiced in the saddle—possibly even has experience in racing or some sort of battle training. The sword she carries is definitely Fae steel and her tattoos are a combination of her people and another race, perhaps elves or giants. Regardless of her storybook infamy, the woman is a hybrid of some type, and an ancient one at that.

A giggle catches my attention and I see Levi gesturing animatedly as his strong thighs grip the horse beneath him. He has zero regard for his safety, especially when he's flirted with someone. The former Snow Queen has captured his attention despite her obvious attachment to Jack and I'm curious what my partner believes is going to happen once we deposit these women in their requested venue. Does he believe they will play with us as others have in the past? We've been on our own since he renounced his title to that dipshit brother of his, but before we left the Sea Kingdom, we were the life of the party.

Being the life of the party forced Levi to give his throne up, but that's another story entirely.

I grunt in annoyance, and the woman in front of me looks over her shoulder. "Comfortable back there, Jorgie? I'm plenty big enough to hold on to."

The frown that crosses my face surprises me. I don't know why that statement bothers me. Jack is not a tiny female, but she's fairly well proportioned and her shape is aesthetically pleasing. Suggesting she's lacking is incorrect, and I wonder briefly why she thinks it is. "I'm doing fine, milady. You handle the steed well."

Her laugh is dark and smoky. It reminds me of the old gentleman's clubs and scotch. "You do *not* have to call me milady. Jack is perfectly acceptable, and Queenie would prefer Elle. We are not the stuffy royals the rest of her court are."

This daring escape with known criminals supports that claim.

"May I ask why you and the former Queen are leaving the Ice Kingdom in secret?" The question may be rude and Levi frequently chides me for not being more mindful of social convention, but something about Jack puts me at ease.

She pauses, turning to face forward as we race through a snowy valley. "I am almost at the end of my service, but I could not leave her in that viper's nest. My exit was not supposed to be a grand plot, but a quiet disappearance when my term was complete."

"The que—Elle is not permitted to leave the kingdom?" I ask in confusion. It's been a long time since I visited my homeland, but even my imperious grandfather wasn't known for forbidding his children or relatives from leaving.

Her entire body tenses up; I feel it. "She has not left her lands since before her parents' death. Currently, she is barely permitted to leave the Summer Palace and certainly not unescorted."

I don't always catch nuance well, but I believe Jack has admitted the Snow Queen has been a prisoner in her realm since she was a child.

"Is that by a decree of the new queen?" I murmur close to her ear.

I do not wish to invade her privacy, but if my suspicions are correct, allowing our words to travel on the wind is dangerous. Even if we are not caught, a skilled elemental mage could recall the sounds from the time we disappeared from the palace.

"Yes. It was never ideal, but since her abdication, the former queen has little in the way of freedom or support besides me. I couldn't leave her to the whims of a woman who might harm her if she felt threatened."

The crest of the hill appears before I can respond. Jack does not react with the same gasp as her companion; that verifies she followed us the last time she saw Levi and I. Both horses come to a stop at the edge of the cliff and I slide off to walk over to aid the queen. Levi arches a brow at me and I shake my head—I will share the information Jack gave me in private.

"We will need to open the field, ladies. The settlement here is protected by goddess magic and we must go through it to get to the ports that your guards do not control."

Jack gives me a curious look, but she nods as she places a few items in the saddlebags of the horses we stole. I don't know who our new friend is framing, but I am certain it's for the best I'm unaware. "I'll send the horses on their way while you tend to your gateway."

Levi watches as I call the phoenix, then turns to Elle. "If you have a cloak in that pack, I would recommend donning it. Your people will recognize you. We must hurry through town to our ship if we want to set sail before your sister blockades the channels we will need to use."

Our mystical friend opens the field surrounding the exiled villagers' town and by the time we are ready to enter, both Jack and Elle have sufficiently disguised themselves. Their horses trot away quickly and when I open my mouth to ask how they will get back to the castle, Jack winks at me. She must have used her own magic to guide them.

It would be nice to know exactly what capabilities they both have, but I'm not sure they trust us enough to reveal that—yet.

AS WE MAKE our way through the village, Elle keeps herself hidden, but the sorrow she's feeling is radiating off of her in waves. She didn't know her sister cleared the towns surrounding the castle of normal citizens to make them appear more prosperous than they are—that much is crystal clear. I hear her sniffle occasionally as a raggedy child or thin farmer scurry past us. Jack is rubbing her back soothingly, but she's also watching for danger. The occasional turn of her head and sharp gaze that fall on the bustling crowd betray her concerns.

She's afraid the people will recognize the former queen and hold her accountable for her sister's sins.

I don't blame her for being suspicious. Levi and I have been here for weeks, helping the encampment grow from tents and refugees to a functioning village, but the people are divided whether Elle is involved in Bella's horrible decrees. They are completely unaware that they have imprisoned the true Snow Queen in the Summer Palace with her companion for years, only to be trotted out at events. Such political scheming is not something regular folks think about and the nasty treatment of a family member wouldn't occur to them, either.

Unfortunately, Elle can't reveal herself and vow to right the wrongs of the current queen unless she wants to remain here, trapped in another prison of her own making. Perhaps if she and Jack escape and can find allies outside of the Ice Kingdom, they can come back to save these poor people. It's simply not an option now and I understand why it would eat at the soft-hearted former queen. In the short time I've known her, she seems like a good person in an unpleasant situation trying to flee an abuser. I'm familiar with abusers and I hate those who prey on the kindhearted.

Maybe I'll come back with Levi and arrange an 'accident' for that lying petty tyrant.

Satisfied with that thought, I close the distance between the ladies and I until Levi and I have them boxed in between us.

It's only a little further to the road that leads to the docks. We hadn't planned on leaving so soon, but the urgency Jack and Elle expressed when they bargained for our help changed our minds. Since we're not sailing with a full crew, we'll need to pick up a few sailors in Tenerife before we head for the Caribbean. I'm sure Levi has already put a call out to some lads who work with us on long journeys. Hopefully, the three I prefer are available.

Beggars can't be choosy, but we are smuggling something more valuable than treasure or goods. The price for the missing queen and her 'kidnappers' will be astronomical.

"Are we getting close?" Jack asks as she navigates through the small marketplace where the merchants trade goods.

Levi plucks two flowers out of a basket, handing the girl carrying them a few coins before presenting one to each of the ladies. "Aye, madame! We're about ten minutes from the port; once we pass the fields up ahead, we turn onto a much less populated road that will take us straight to the sea."

The former queen turns slightly, and I can see under the large hood of her cloak. She looks nervous as she looks at Jack. "I haven't been on a boat since I was very little. You'll all have to forgive me as I acclimate to the new things. I'll do my best not to be a burden."

I blink, watching Jack and Levi offer her their arms. They're both treating her as if she's fragile, but I don't believe that's accurate. It takes incredible strength to admit the things she has and then to forge ahead into the unknown despite immense danger. Elle has a heart of velvet and a spine of obsidian; she need not apologize for learning new things.

"Ah. She's getting under your skin," Jack says as she leans towards me. "Trust me, I know how it works."

My brow furrows and I roll my eyes, stomping ahead of the three of them towards the road to the docks. Her assertion is utter poppycock—it took me months to warm up to my current companion. Despite his obvious gifts in the bedroom, he's flighty, spoiled, and incapable of focusing for more than a few minutes. It's like having a hyperactive golden retriever with me at all times, which didn't become endearing for quite a while.

Besides, I have more important things to worry about than whether they are giving the former queen her due. I have to keep us all alive.

II

HE'S A PIRATE

JACK

THE SHIP IS PRETTY FANCY FOR A DUO OF RAGTAG pirates. I suppose I shouldn't be surprised given Levi's revelation that his father is the *God of the fucking Sea*, but he's clearly not part of that court at the moment, so...

Once we were safely away from land, Jorgie explained we would need to make a stop to gather more crew members before heading to our destination. I have experience on the open ocean from my time with my rum-swigging pirate ex, so I understood, but Elle is still nervous. The Canary Islands have a rich piratical history and Tenerife is probably packed with fairy tale and supe creatures. It's a gateway to the rest of the Atlantic and I imagine many of the folks who live there are part-time seafarers—for a price.

Luckily, I have several life debt items that require those who are servants of the ocean to pay tribute in my magic pouch. My time with the Captain, though brief, ended on friendly terms and we had many adventures that make me an important name in that world. I didn't need to use them to influence Levi or Jorgie, but I will if it helps us gain the sailors we require for our long voyage.

That tidbit will probably come out anyway once I'm seen without a hood and the boys will be shocked as hell.

I went by a different name in my pirate days. It was another time when I was hiding out from my heritage by seeking asylum with a wealthy British governor. He needed respectability, and I needed a safe port to weather the storm after my ill-fated relationship with Galen. It worked out well until a band of pirates came into the picture and they kidnapped me.

To be honest, it was one of the best times in my life until now and I don't regret a second of it. I miss the men I collected back then, particularly my mercurial, cursed captain. Nothing lasts forever though, and none of them made fairytale status, so they eventually died. I attended their funerals in disguise and I've kept everything he willed to me close ever since. His compass is one of my most treasured possessions.

"Jackie?" Queenie comes up behind me as I gaze out into the sea. "Are you sure this detour is safe? "

"No, but I've been to pirate colonies before. If we respect their traditions, we should be able to get the crew and leave before anything bad happens."

I can sense her frown as she rests her cheek on my bare shoulder blade. "I trust you. Levi and Jorgie seem to be men we can put our faith in as well, but I have little to no experience with men since the failed engagement."

Ah, the former suitor who betrayed her. I would have liked to destroy him, but he was long gone when I came into the picture.

Turning to pull her into my arms, I brush the wisps of hair off her forehead. We changed out of our finery once the ship was out of port and now we're both in comfortable clothes. We scrubbed our faces clean of the heavy makeup and I braided her hair to keep it out of her way. Queenie looks younger like this, though as immortals, our aging stops at the point we gain unending vitality. The heart stopping thing is her eyes—the weight of sorrow that always filled them has lessened and it makes her almost glow.

"I won't ever let anyone hurt you, love. You can count on that." My lips brush the top of her head and she squeezes me tight.

"No one told me there were hugs! I want a hug," Levi pouts as he approaches and I roll my eyes. This guy.

Q lifts her head and arches a brow at him. "What have you done that deserves a hug, pirate?"

His pout grows, and I can feel her defenses weaken. She likes him, but she knows better than to trust anyone who hasn't proven themselves now.

"I helped you and your bossy lover escape the clutches of an evil queen. I think that deserves a little credit, right?" He bats his lashes adorably and I sigh.

Danger zone, thy name is Levi.

My girl pretends to think about it, then nods slowly. "That might qualify. But it also means Jorgie should receive one as well."

"Jorgie surrenders his to Levi," the dark-haired captain of the ship mutters as he passes us on the way to adjust a sail.

"More for me!" Levi claps his hands before holding his arms out.

"For fuck's sake..." I mutter.

Queenie glared at Jorgie's back, then strides over to Levi and gives him one of her trademark irresistible embraces. She hugs like she's trying to absorb all of your pain and sorrow with her limbs—it's addictive as hell. There's no way he doesn't feel the warmth that emanates from my Ice Queen as she squeezes him.

He beams when she finally lets go. "Holy shit, your Highness. I mean, Elle... you give the best hugs I've ever..."

Chuckling, I wink at him. "No shit."

A grunt and huff from the mast make me smirk to myself. Bet that grumpy fucker wishes he hadn't rejected his half of the offer now. He's been distant and irritable since we set sail; I thought he was focused on the ship. Obviously, that wasn't correct. The pirate with unknown origins and a soft spot for his first mate is purposefully trying not to engage with us.

Interesting... we'll see how long that lasts with my girl flitting about.

"Oh, for the love of stinky yeti feet, Levi. You'll have to come up with something else to call me." Queenie sighs and shakes her head. "No one calls me Elle—not even my sister—and I definitely don't want to be called any version of your Highness or Majesty. I haven't been a monarch in over a decade; it doesn't feel right."

"Jack calls you Queenie," Jorgie points out. "How is that different?"

I snort, tugging her back into my arms and putting my chin on her head. "That is information you are not privy to unless you've been in our bedroom, Captain."

"If that's an invitation..."

The giggle that follows his bobbing brows makes me smile. Q may not realize she's flirting with the sea shifter, but she's a natural at it. I tilt my head at him, narrowing my gaze. "When I issue an invitation to my bed, you don't have to question it."

Before Levi can retort, Jorgie stomps by and grabs his shoulder. "Come on, lover boy. We have duties to attend to. The GPS says we're only an hour or two from making land in Tenerife."

"To be continued..."

Rolling my eyes at the flirtatious sailor, I wait until they disappear into the cabin to look at my girl. It's time for a discussion about what's happening and what we're comfortable with. Given the behavior of our current crew members, I don't think it can wait.

"Love, let's go up on the forecastle deck and have a chat. I think we need to discuss the tentacled pirate in the room."

She nods, smiling up at me. "I'll go anywhere with you, Jackie. You didn't have to help me for all of those years or risk the wrath of my sister by bringing me with you. There's nothing in the world I wouldn't do for you."

I take her hand, leading her up the stairs to the front deck carefully. "That doesn't mean you owe me, darling. At first, I was doing a job because I was paid, but eventually, you wormed your way into my heart. Now everything I do is because I care about you—I don't want you to go from one controlling relationship to another. You are your own person and you can make your decisions. I don't have to agree, but we have to talk about them like adults."

She frowns and tilts her head. "What decisions are we talking about? I didn't leave only because you asked me to, if it's that. I came with you when I realized that showing up for yourself sometimes means leaving people behind who don't give you the same respect. The delusional version of me Bella has coaxed her court and everyone else into seeing? I can't control that; I can only be who I am and live my truth. If they choose to accept her self-centered ramblings, I don't need them."

Whoa. What the hell metamorphosis has my girl gone through since we made this crazy plan?

"Damn, woman. That was almost inspiring." I chuckle softly and stroke my hand over her cheek. "But you're not wrong. All of that is true, but what I wanted to ask you about is much different."

"Then what?"

I pause, considering how to word this so I don't hurt her feelings unintentionally. "It's been us against the world for a long time. I have a lot of experience with various types of relationships in the past, as you know..."

Queenie pulls back and rolls her eyes at me. "Jackie, I'm aware of that. If you're asking if the boys interest me, the answer is yes. I mean, not more than you, of course, but... I've been sheltered for so long. I don't have your past, nor anything to compare to outside of us. I think they might be kind of perfect to experiment with if they are agreeable. Don't you?"

I'm pretty sure my face looks like someone smacked me with a brick right now.

"I... uh..." Clearing my throat, I shake the cobwebs out of my brain and take a deep breath. "I agree, my love. I would like to explore that as well. It's not like we're going to see them after we arrive in the Caribbean and long sea voyages are boring as hell without a little skin slapping."

Her lips curve into a tiny smirk and she whispers, "Did I hear Levi has tentacles? Like in one of the Japanese cartoons?"

The laugh that escapes me booms over the deck, and I nod. "Yes, love. Exactly like that."

"Then I'm definitely game. I always wondered what all the fuss was. And we don't even know what the grumpy gus is packing! This is so exciting!"

Oh, this is going to be a fucking mess, but luckily, that's my specialty.

ALMÁCIGA STILL BEARS evidence of the long past volcanic eruption on its black sand beach. It's on the less tourist-y side of Tenerife and close to where we could take a cable car to El Teide, the mountain in the middle of the island. Jorgie and Levi asked us to stay in the beach area while they travelled to a local fishing village where their fellow ne'er-do-wells are likely to be found during the day. I'm not sure where they go at night, but the emphasis on daytime makes me believe they have some sort of pirate pub or hideaway.

Regardless, I was fine with taking Queenie to the row of shops and buying us a few necessities for tropical life. We had little in the way of warm weather clothing we could shove in our packs and once we gave my card a spanking, I felt more at ease.

We grabbed drinks and some delicious smelling Spanish food after we dumped our haul on the ship, then headed for the beach in scandalously small swimsuits. Q was like a kid in a candy store, marveling over every new experience, and I indulged her. She's had a lot of pain and sorrow in her lifetime and I want to excise it from her brain.

"It was so lovely to choose my clothing!" Her smile is bright as she looks at me from behind large, sparkling sunglasses. "Colors besides blue and white, pants and shorts, dresses that don't weigh a hundred pounds... oh, I can't wait to wear it all!"

I ruffle her hair and lead her to a spot near the crystal blue waves of the Atlantic. Spreading the blanket out, I kick off my sandals and put my feet in the waves. She follows suit, wiggling her toes with glee. "It's good to see you so happy."

"I am! Of course I'm worried about being found, but I plan to enjoy every second of my freedom, no matter what." She reaches into the bag I purchased and pulls out the new phone. I got her with a devilish grin. "I have my own phone now. Smile quickly so I can make my background picture of you looking beautiful in this scenery."

Rolling my eyes, I lean back on my hands and smile at her as she snaps away. I can't tell her no—this is her first phone, and she's as excited as a teenager. "I got a new chip for mine as well, just in case someone tries to track us."

"Excellent. Now finish your food while I walk around and take photos like a silly girl."

The sounds of sand and surf are soothing while I watch her stroll along the waterline, snapping selfies and landscapes happily. It's hard to believe that three weeks ago, I was planning to leave her behind and take off on my own. It would have been the worst decision I'd ever made, and I've made some doozies. The entire Internet is aware of my monumentally bad life choices, and this trip is all about leaving that legacy behind.

Once she's done playing with her new toy, we take a dip in the ocean, splashing about in the waves. The guys have been gone a few hours now and though I'm not concerned, I keep my eyes peeled for signs of anyone watching us too closely. I don't think they'd give us up for a fat wad of cash, but they are pirates.

Who knows what kind of nonsense they may have gotten up to before landing in the Ice Kingdom?

Queenie floats by on her back, her limbs stretched out like a starfish as she sighs. "This is so relaxing. I hope this is what you have planned for our Caribbean future."

"Absolutely," I reply. "Sun, sand, surf, and drinks with tiny umbrellas forever, darling."

A rumble in the distance distracts me, and I stare out at the ocean. The wind kicks up a bit, making the wisps of hair around my face flutter. I tilt my head and scent the air—something about that sound feels familiar, but I can't place it.

"What's wrong?" Q asks. She stops floating and paddles over to me as I study our surroundings quietly.

"Nothing. The weather may be turning. We should head for shore." She nods and we both swim towards shore, shaking off water as we make our way to our things. I let her pack up the blanket and our trash, still unsure why the atmosphere feels charged around us.

"Should we walk down the beach toward the pier so we're closer to the ship? If it rains, we'll be able to make a run for it."

"I think so," I murmur.

Strolling along the coastline, a bolt of lightning cracks out over the waves and I frown. It's not the best time of year for the beach going to Tenerife, but it's past the storm season. When we paid at the clothing shop, I realized it was New Year's Eve, so I checked the web after installing my new SIM. We've been gone for almost a week without a single mention of our absence on social media. A sudden storm makes me suspicious that our brief respite from being hunted may be at an end.

The new queen may not have magic, but she certainly has access to those who do.

I pick up the pace, walking faster towards the pier. There's no need to alarm Queenie, but I have a bad feeling suddenly. Before I can turn to tell her to get on the ship, I trip over something sticking out of the ground and go flying face first into the black sand.

"What the actual fuck?" I mutter as I push up, spitting out the grit in my mouth. "What was that?"

"Jack, are you okay?!"

The shout makes me grunt with irritation. I know that means Levi and Jorgie have returned in time to see me wipe out like a fool. Queenie holds her hand out and I get to a sitting position before they get to us. I pick up the weird-looking bottle I tripped over with a snarl, then glance up at the veritable smorgasbord of attractive people looking at me in concern.

Why is all of my humiliation public? I must be cursed.

"Who the hell are all these guys?" I snarl.

Levi beams at me, looking like the sea shifter that swallowed a boat full of victims. "Our crew, of course!" He points to each one, then rattles off. "This is Ace, Dash, and Kael."

I squint at three men, wondering how two ridiculously good looking pirates found three more impossibly attractive me to sign on to a voyage that could land them all in prison. "Nice to meet you, I guess?"

Kael gives me a shy smile. He has wide, dark eyes and wavy black hair with olive skin. "What did you in, ma'am?"

Oh, hell no.

"First... It's Jack. Second, I don't know what the hell this thing is." I hold up the bottle, studying it for a moment, when I realize it has something inside. I frown as I work to get the cork out, growling softly when it seems to be lodged in there right.

"Let me," the blond surfer Levi called Dash offers. "My hands are super strong. Comes from my off-season job."

"If you say so," I mutter, handing him the bottle. I hate men who want to rescue women, but he seems sincere enough. I don't think he's patronizing me.

"He's a masseuse at the resorts when he isn't sailing," Jorgie supplies with a smirk.

Damn him. He knew why I was being salty.

"That I am." Dash grips the bottle with one hand and it immediately shifts into a bird-like claw and he pops it out without fanfare. "Ah-ha!"

Snatching it back, I eye him warily, then the other two. "What the hell are you guys, anyway?"

Ace finally pays attention. He's been staring at me and the ocean behind me silently the entire time. While Dash is sun-kissed and Kael is dark, Ace seems to shimmer with a rainbow of colors. His hair, his skin... even his eyes have multi-colored flecks. "As if that is what's important at the moment. Ugh. Dash is a griffin, Kael is a cheetah shifter, and I'm mer-folk. See what's in the damn bottle?"

Jorgie remains quiet, but he arches a brow at me encouragingly.

Fine, if he doesn't want to share, I'll figure out what has me sprawled on my ass in the sand.

"Hurry, Jackie, the suspense is killing me!" Queenie whispers.

I turn the bottle over and an old piece of parchment falls out, rolling across my lap like a decree at the castle. "It's a map."

Levi grabs it and holds it up, his expression almost joyous. "Oh, it's not just a map." He turns it for all of us to see. "This is a treasure map."

"Fuck me." Jorgie glares at me as if I've committed a grievous sin and runs his hand through his hair. "Not again."

Even Ace looks chagrined, and I don't know why. "Why the long faces, guys? It's probably a tourist trap leftover from some booze cruise."

"No way! Look how old it is!" Levi bounces over to show Queenie, and I can tell by the look on her face she's catching his enthusiasm.

"The weather," Kael says solemnly as he looks around us. "Ace, you need to check it."

"Hold up. What's wrong with the weather and why does Ace need to examine it?" I push to my feet, putting my hands on my hips as I glare at them. "Stop talking around me."

Jorgie holds his hand out, and Levi gives him the map reluctantly. "This is an area around the Triangle, Ace. Take it and see if Kael is right."

The merman sighs dramatically and takes the parchment, walking over to the sea so it laps at his feet. "Reveal thy bounty!"

"Ooh, this is so exciting!" Q grabs my arm and holds on as we watch the sparkling pirate grasp the paper and hold it up in the air.

The sun peeks out from behind a cloud, a single ray hitting the yellowed map, and it glows. A wave shoots into the air nearby, then another, until there's a row of water spouts lined up in front us. When I turn to gape at Levi and Jorgie in amazement, I find Levi glowing as well, tentacles waving around him in excitement. Ace groans and drops his arms as he spins around with a defeated expression on his pretty face.

"Well, Levi, once again you've thrown us in the shit, bro."

Jorgie grimaces. "As I feared."

"I enjoy them," Kael says with a small grin.

That's it.

Fury wells up inside of me and I feel the magic I button up release as my size increases until I'm in my true form. Towering over them, I boom, "*Tell me what it is before I smash you all into smithereens!*"

Queenie's laugh tinkles in the air as she watches me fondly. "Lesson one in dating a hybrid giantess, gentleman. Try not to piss her off enough to lose control of her form. It's a little intimidating at first."

Their mouths hang open but no one speaks so I shout again, *"Are you hard of hearing?"*

"No," Jorgie says calmly. "But you should control your temper better. Not all of us are lesser beings, Jacqueline. I'd prefer not to feel I need to defend my men."

I crack my neck and breathe deeply, using the same steps I taught Queenie to quench my ire. When I shrink to my normal size, Levi gives me a wink and Kael smiles. I wait, fuming silently as they ignore my demands. Finally, Jorgie nods at Ace and he holds the map up to show the completed picture on it.

"It means Levi's father has given us a quest and our trip to the Caribbean is no longer a holiday. A god has conscripted us."

Motherfucker. I have the worst luck in the cosmos.

REVIEWS

If you have enjoyed this book, please leave reviews! It helps other readers find our work, which helps us as indie authors.
Thank you!

You can add reviews for Hoist the Flag on the following platforms:

Amazon
Goodreads
Bookbub

GRATUITOUS SHOUT-OUTS

BEING AN INDIE AUTHOR IS A HOUSE OF CARDS IF YOU DON'T HAVE THE PROPER SUPPORT, AND I WANT TO THANK EVERYONE WHO HAS BEEN THERE FOR ME THIS YEAR.

Thank you to my alphas, betas, ARC, and street teams. Without you, I wouldn't be able to focus on my writing and get as many books out for you as possible.

Merci to my family. Not everyone has a kiddo and spouse who put up with your crazy deadlines and needy creative stuff 24/7, even when it means a surprise therapy puppy. Also to my parents who have been supporting this dream in their own way since COVID shut my store down. I couldn't do it without you, either. Even my asshole brother trades memes with me at all hours of the day to help me blow off steam. Thanks for being the favorite, buddy; it made me work harder.

Gracias to my amazing friends, both online and off. Whether I talk with you every day or every couple of weeks, allowing me to vent or making me laugh is *everything* when times get hard. Serenity, Sarah, Melanie, Brit, and all the rest—I'd shank a bitch for you...right in the kidney, no questions asked.

Danke to my readers—the ones who make it possible to continue pursuing my dream of writing full time. Your support, your kind words, your reviews, and the fact that you keep showing up, no matter how tight my deadline is or how long I made this damn book... that is the stuff dreams are made of.

About the Author

Cassandra
FEATHERSTONE

Cassandra Featherstone has been writing since she could hold a pencil.

She wrote her first story about a girl picking strawberries when she was three and has been creating worlds in her head ever since. After winning multiple awards for essays, poems, short stories and a very cheesy academy romance novel in high school, they selected her to attend the prestigious Governors School for the Arts in high school.

Her love of the arts is vast: she plays three instruments and marched flute/piccolo for six years), took ten years of tap/jazz/ballet/tumbling, and sang/acted major roles in many musicals and plays. She auditioned for a slew of colleges, but selected NYU for musical theater and lived in NYC for several years while she was in the studio.

After meeting her husband, she moved back to the Midwest and eventually spawned her mini-me, affectionately known as the goblin.

She has worked in many industries, from banking to retail management and, most recently, a decade in multiple positions at an indie bookstore until COVID-19 permanently closed her educational services department.

Cassandra is passionate about literacy, but when she picked up her laptop to write her first published novel in March 2020, she focused on subjects that not only spoke to her soul, but affected many of the women she'd met throughout her twisty life path.

Bullying, PTSD, body dysmorphia, mental illness, reinvention, and claiming your space are frequent themes in her books, as well as respectful, non-fetishized representation of LGBTQIA+ relationships. Her expansion of the reverse harem genre to include various types of polycules and diverse characters with three-dimensional personalities, hopes, and dreams was less common when she first published, but to her delight, becoming a standard reader request in the current atmosphere.

Because of her personal experiences in middle and high school, Cassandra is a staunch defender of those who get targeted by those with actual or perceived power that attack those who don't.

She's also affectionately known as the Muppet for her outrageous, extroverted personality and her wacky brand of theater kid social media posts and videos.

Cassandra lives in the Midwest/South with her computer geek husband, artsy college goblin, an author dog, and five cats that Loki himself spawned. Her works include sci-fi fantasy/urban fantasy, paranormal, humorous, contemporary, and academy whychoose/polyam romances with characters over eighteen. Her books never include non-consensual elements, but feature accurate, safe depictions of BDSM and kink lifestyles.

READ MORE AT CASSANDRA'S WEBSITE OR HER FACEBOOK PAGE. SIGN UP FOR EXCLUSIVE CONTENT AND UPDATES HERE.

FIND HER ON ANY OF THE SOCIAL MEDIA BELOW AS SHE *LOVES* TO CHAT AND *NEVER* SLEEPS!

ALSO BY CASSANDRA FEATHERSTONE

THE MISFIT PROTECTION PROGRAM SERIES

Road to the Hollow

Return to the Hollow

Home to the Hollow

Rejected in the Hollow

Revealed in the Hollow

AUDIO OF THE MISFIT PROTECTION PROGRAM SERIES *(coming soon!)*

Road to the Hollow

Return to the Hollow

Roused in the Hollow

Rejected in the Hollow

VILLAINS & VIXENS

Bloodthirsty (Book One)

Ruthless (Book Two)

AUDIO OF THE VILLAINS & VIXENS SERIES *(coming soon!)*

Bloodthirsty

Ruthless

TRIANGLES & TRIBULATIONS

Hoist the Flag (PQ) in Jingle My Balls

Yo-Ho Holes (Book One)

COVEN OF THE SERPENT

Daughters of Hecate (Book One)

CHILDREN OF THE MOON- WITH SERENITY RAYNE

New Moon Rising (Book One) (Preorder now!)

THE APEX SOCIETY CAPERS

Come Out and Prey

Let Us Prey

In Prey We Trust (Pre-order now!)

ANTHOLOGIES

Unwritten

Shifters Unleashed

(featuring 'Hell on Wheels')

Jingle My Balls

(Featuring 'Hoist the Flag')

Love is in the Air

(Featuring 'Reunion in the Hollow' with Serenity Rayne)

Of Seas and Storms (2024)

CODENAME: THE RIFT SERIES

Special Edition of Codename: The Rift

Special Edition of A New World Order

The Alpha & The Omega

Trials of the Beast (Winter 2024)

Book Five (Winter 2025)

Book Six (Tentative Fall 2026)

Book Seven (Tentative Spring 2027)

Book Eight (Tentative Fall 2028)

THE EARLY YEARS PREQUELS

An Investigative Tour of 'The Company' Starring Delilah L. O'Hara, Part One (Only available in the Special Edition of Codename: The Rift)*

An Investigative Tour of 'The Company' Starring Delilah L. O'Hara, Part Two (Only available in the Special Edition of A New World Order)*

The Caravan (Coming Winter 2023)

Into the Wilde

*The Escape Plan (Newsletter Sign-up Exclusive)**

Hubris (Coming Winter 2024)

The Old Switcheroo (Coming Summer 2024)

Baby Steps (Coming Fall 2025)

Situation F.U.B.A.R (Coming Winter 2024)

The Beast Speaks (Coming Winter 2025)

THE WINTER PREQUELS

The Beast Rising: The Riftverse Prequels Boxed Set

(Contains: Diary of Genesis, Delilah, Forgiveness, A Twisted Path, and The Beginning)

THE CLAW ENFORCEMENT CHRONICLES

Call the Magickal Midwife

All in the Family (Coming Spring 2024)

THE SIDE QUESTS

Hallelujah

Trial by Fire (Coming Winter 2025)

The Kitty Does Halloween

The Beast, The Maiden, and The Perfect Present